Susan R. E. Wall lives in Portsmouth, England. She founded her own company in 2003 providing bookkeeping and financial management service to proprietors of small to medium-sized businesses. Married since 1987 to Bill – her soulmate; together they have a wonderful daughter, Kathryn.

A passion for romance and storytelling led Susan to bring her most treasured possession, being a box of some more than 60 love letters between her parents, to life. It began as a project to simply collate the memorabilia she had inherited into a narrative for her daughter, as sadly, she never knew her grandparents.

My husband, Bill, and daughter, Kathryn, who continually encouraged me with this work. My sister, Marietta, who went through so much as a young child. To the incredibly special 'American Friends', the Meyer-Ekberg family who were so extraordinarily kind to my mother; something she was always eternally grateful for.

Susan R. E. Wall

TRUE LOVE CONQUERS ALL

AUSTIN MACAULEY PUBLISHERS™

LONDON * CAMBRIDGE * NEW YORK * SHARJAH

A CIP catalogue record for this title is available from the British Library.

ISBN 9781528936033 (Paperback)
ISBN 9781398410350 (ePub e-book)

www.austinmacauley.com

First Published (2021)
Austin Macauley Publishers Ltd
25 Canada Square
Canary Wharf
London
E14 5LQ

Chapter 1

Life, overall, has been good to me. But as I approach my 91st birthday, I am not in the best of health. Currently, I am residing in a hospital. I do not think there can be a more depressing place than being stuck in a hospital bed, in an EMI (elderly, mental and infirm) unit, surrounded by coffin dodgers, all of whom seem to be knocking at death's door.

I am here because I slipped and managed to break not only my hip but also my wrist. Osteoporosis was diagnosed several years ago, and I have always tried to be as careful as possible. But my passion for wooden floors and then lots of rugs was to be my downfall – apologies for the pun! My family have tried and tried to get me to take up the rugs, but I loved them and wanted to continue to admire them until I was no longer able to. So, some years ago, I arranged for all the rugs to be firmly secured to the floor. But, despite this, I tripped over the edge of one.

I had never had to use my personal alarm before and, as much as I protested about having one, it was a lifesaver. I managed to press it and almost instantly, an operator was talking to me through the base unit in my hallway. Having briefly explained my predicament they immediately arranged for an ambulance to come to my assistance and for my neighbour, the wonderful Betty, to be contacted as she had a key. Everyone duly arrived on cue and I was uplifted, put on a stretcher and carted off to hospital. And here I remain.

My body may have packed up, but the brain is still as active as ever. You would not think so though considering the way some jumped up healthcare assistant spoke to me this morning. So condescending and as though I was two halfpennies short of a shilling: leaning over me, speaking loudly and announcing her words at a snail's pace. Then to cap it all, she kept calling me dear. As I do not have antlers and have always hated being referred to as dear, I was not impressed. Not many years ago, I would have probably spoken my mind and put her in her place. But now, I just cannot be bothered.

It is a small ward consisting of eight beds. All the occupants are oldies like me and in various states of decay. The nursing staff busily go about their daily routines. Try as they might, it is obvious that they cannot always do so. But they make a good effort, and I am being well looked after.

So, here I am, lying in God's waiting room, expecting his calling card at any moment. It will not be much longer now. My time on this earth will soon be at an end.

The trouble with getting old is the likelihood that you will spend most of your time alone, waiting for the inevitable and it gives you far too much time to reflect on a long life. If I were asked to sum up my life in one word it would be 'eventful'. There are probably a few synonyms I could use but this one word seems the most appropriate.

There are so many memories, which would be expected when you reach my ripe old age, and sometimes I find myself immersed in deep thought and wondering did all I remember occur or has my love of literature clouded my recollections. It all seems so long ago. I play games in my head trying to get the memories in order.

The more I think, the more I recall. But it is strange how the memory can be selective. Often, something I remember suddenly triggers another memory from quite a different time. Then comes the difficulty in trying to fathom whether it did happen or is my brain playing tricks again.

My life has, as I have said, been eventful and I felt that my experiences should be documented: warts and all. I am a product of an era when so much happened in the world and it would be a shame if, on my passing, my life and experiences were all too quickly forgotten.

My next-door neighbour Betty's grandson, Jamie, came up with a "wicked idea" as he called it. Rheumatoid arthritis in my hands makes it nigh on impossible to hold a pen let alone write and a few years ago, he suggested I buy a digital voice recorder. It is quite simple to use with big buttons and I can easily manage to turn it on and off. He knows that I struggle to recall memories and when I do think of something relevant, all too easily it quickly disappears into the ether of what is left of my brain, maybe never to be heard of again. The gadget enabled me to record voice notes, which I can playback to jolt the memory once again. I was sceptical, as I am not at all into these new fancy electronics. But, as the months passed, he proved himself to be right and the machine has been a Godsend.

I have been making recordings for a couple of years now and, with his help, I have been able to get them in some semblance of order. He has then transcribed the notes into a sort of diary which is the basis of what I am trying to pull together here. My ultimate wish is that my memories and experiences are documented so that my descendants can pass on my life story. We all know that generally upon death, all too easily and quickly, memories and experiences invariably disappear forever.

To go hand in hand with the diary is my most treasured and cherished possession: a box of letters between me and the love of my life, my dearest darling John. Most were written whilst we were courting (a wonderful expression which is rarely used now) together with a number after we married. It is because of these letters that I felt the need to tell my story so that they could be shared and appreciated by others. Letter writing is, sadly, more or less, a thing of the past. Years ago, it used to be such an important aspect of our lives. It is a bygone art form that permitted so much to be expressed: one's feelings, the warmth of friendship, apologies, desires, hatreds; a multitude of expression.

But now, with technology, it has been superseded by emails or texts. As a signed-up member of the older generation, much as I try to embrace new innovations, I think that it is a shame that rarely do people correspond in hand-written missives. The letters are truly remarkable but before we get to them, I want to put my life in perspective and explain what eventually led me to meet, fall deeply in love with and marry the absolute love of my life, my darling John.

And so, it begins.

I met John in 1953. However, I think it would be sensible to talk about my ancestry and life before I met him. What I do not want though is for my ramblings to be a political or historical piece of writing. So much has already been written about this time in our world history. So, I will detail some of my personal observations and how some incidents affected my life and not give a factually based history lesson.

First revelation – I am German.

My parents (papa and mutti) were Paul and Herta Schild and they had been childhood sweethearts.

Paul was born on 11 December 1887 and named Paul Richard Max Schild. Paul had been born in Berlin but due to economic pressures, his family had moved in the same year to Oderberg.

Herta was born on 26th January 1892, named Herta Freida Olga Rössel. This was in Wartin, Kreis Randow in the district of Casekow. The village was small and located in the northeast of Germany about 128 km from Berlin. As with Paul's parents, Helga's parents also relocated to Oderberg as there were better job opportunities.

The small town of Oderberg lies on the banks of the River Oder and is around 55 km northeast of Berlin and not far from the border with Poland. It was the most picturesque of towns surrounded by mountains, lakes and forests. The area was sparsely populated and with little industry apart from the boatyards and sawmills. It was in a sawmill that both of my grandpapas worked. Their respective families were awfully close and relied on each other as it was generally a hard life for them. As Paul and Herta became closer, it was a great joy and comfort for both families, and they could not have been happier.

It was expected that Paul would follow his papa, into the sawmill. But he decided at quite a young age that he wanted to do something different. It was much to the consternation of his parents that he persuaded the local butcher/slaughter man to take him on as an apprentice. So, at 15 he began the arduous work. He knew he was still too young to marry but his intention was that as soon as he was able, he would settle down and marry his sweetheart, Herta.

Because of the relatively close proximity to Berlin and as the surrounding area to Oderberg was incredibly beautiful, even in those days at the turn of the 20th century, the town was a tourist attraction. During the summer months, the weekly train service to and from Berlin became daily and tourists would arrive to go walking in the mountains. This influx was also a time when a bit more money could be earned. Although rudimentary maps of the area were available, tourists liked to have a local guide. So, never one to miss an opportunity, Paul would act as a guide when he was not required by Herr Grunewald, the butcher. Of course, while this was a great source of additional income it also gave Paul the opportunity to talk to the tourists about his passion, which was Berlin.

Much had changed in Berlin since his parents left there. Paul dreamed of being able to visit and although it was relatively close it may well have been 500 km away. But, by chatting to the holidaymakers, his dreams seemed to be that much closer. He yearned to see the bright lights and experience the hustle and bustle of the city. He had heard so much about Potsdamerplatz, Alexanderplatz, numerous horse-drawn carriages, trolleybuses, Wertheim department store,

Kaiser Willem's statue and Kurfürstendamm. But these were pipe dreams. He did not think he would ever be able to witness these visions for himself.

When he started his apprenticeship in 1902, his wages were minimal, and he knew he had no hope whatsoever of marrying Herta for some considerable time. But, eventually, after a few years of savings, they were able to marry and settled down to life in Oderberg.

Sadly, their happiness was not to last. World War 1 was to intervene.

World War One, also known as the First World War or the Great War, was a global war originating in Europe that lasted from 28 July 1914 to 11 November 1918. Contemporaneously described as 'the war to end all wars'; it led to the mobilisation of more than 70 million military personnel, including 60 million Europeans, making it one of the largest wars in history. It is also one of the deadliest conflicts in history, with an estimated nine million combatant and seven million civilian deaths as a direct result of the war.

Apart from the great need for timber, initially, their lives in Oderberg were relatively untouched by the ravages of war. The tourists had stopped coming at the onset of war so that meant they lost the additional income. However, Herta managed to find work as a housekeeper for a local businessman. These few extra Marks made a huge difference to their income and kept the wolf from the door.

The first couple of years went by without much of an impact for Paul, Herta and their respective families but that was about to change. Paul was called up to join the German Army. He was at the time around 26 years old so it was no surprise that he would have to participate.

Herta was left alone and obviously worried that she might never see Paul again.

The winter of 1916 was harsh and rationing began. The shortages made life difficult and the community became disheartened.

As is always the case in these circumstances, it is the poor who suffer the most. Coal was in short supply but with all the timber around, at least they would not be cold.

The news of the war was also not encouraging. At first, the feeling was that, without a doubt, Germany would conquer all and be victorious. But, when France did not simply capitulate, the morale of the population began to diminish. Newspapers were full of crime, tales of scandal and corruption. By early 1918, Berlin was the centre of crippling strikes mostly led by the Communists and Socialists.

Thankfully, Paul survived and returned to Oderberg, Herta and their families.

Personal-Ausweis

für den ...

der **5. Kompagnie Armierungs-Bataillon 63.**

Personal-Beschreibung:

Groesse: ... Gestalt: ... Nase: ... Haar: ...

Bart: ... besondere Kennzeichen: ...

Geboren: ...

Eigenhaendige Unterschrift ... U. den ...

Feldw.-Ltnt. u. Komp.-Fuehrer.

Paul Schild Ausweis 19th September 1918

At the end of WW1, Germany was in utter turmoil. Herr Grunewald was still not able to take back Paul. Therefore, Paul decided that he needed to make a better life for himself and Herta, and Berlin was the starting point.

Chapter 2

Paul and Herta started to make plans to relocate to Berlin. Although born in Berlin, Paul had no living relations there. However, they were fortunate that before the war they had befriended a couple who were regular tourists, Herr and Frau Schneider (a childless couple) who had said that, if ever they could make it to Berlin, they would assist them with accommodation and work. Paul and Herta had no idea if Herr and Frau Schneider were still living at the same address they had given them, but with little reason to stay in Oderberg, they made up their minds, much to the family's objections, to go and find out. They had little savings, and the family came up with a few Marks that would just be enough to get them to Berlin and sustain them for a month. If they were not successful, they would have no choice but to return to Oderberg.

And so it was that, in early August 1919, the couple made their way to Oderberg Hauptbahnhof (central station). As a close family, everyone came to the station to wish the couple a good journey. It was quite an event in the small town. Rarely did anyone leave, especially on what was thought to be such a perilous journey. But, despite the reservations that everyone seemed to have, they were determined. In some respects, I think it was Paul who was the driving force; Herta was quite timid, and I am sure she just followed along agreeing with whatever Paul suggested. She would have genuinely believed that whatever he recommended would be with their best interests at heart.

The couple left their cherished town with much apprehension. They had no idea what they were going to find once they arrived in Berlin. It could be that all they aspired to would so easily be knocked back in one simple hit if, when they arrived, the Schneiders were nowhere to be found. Also, to make their decision even harder was the fact that Herta was pregnant – with me! They had kept this fact secret from the family because they knew that if they were aware, they would have undoubtedly never have given their blessings or helped in any way to fulfil their dreams.

All their possessions were packed in two small suitcases. They also had a knapsack with provisions for the journey. And that was it. Their whole life amounted to so little but their love for one another knew no bounds and with happy hearts, they waved goodbye to everyone, tears cascading down their cheeks, onwards to what they hoped would be a fruitful new life.

Several hours later the train finally pulled in to Lehrter Stadtbahnhof; they had reached their destination. They got off the train and were immediately completely in awe of their surroundings. Right away, the one thing that struck them was the noise and hustle and bustle. In Oderberg, life was not so frantic; everyone took their time. Here, it was the complete reverse. People were racing to and fro, and the noise was, to them, quite deafening. But this was nothing to what they were going to experience once they left the confines of the station.

This was an impressive city, but a city going through incredible change. The January 1919 uprising (Spartakusaufstand) was a general strike and its suppression marked the end of the German revolution. The Weimar Republic had just been formed. This was the parliamentary republic established to replace the Imperial form of government and named after the city where the constitutional assembly took place. Although known as the Deutsche Reich, it was generally known as Germany (Deutschland). It was the beginning of a period of utter turmoil for Germany. The Republic came under threat from left and right-wing sources, both committing atrocious violent acts in many German cities, resulting in numerous deaths.

General strikes occurred in the Ruhr region and in other major industrial areas which crippled the already fragile economy. The awful situation was exacerbated by hyperinflation. With no goods to trade and striking workers being paid by the state, a solution the government came up with was to print additional currency. This currency was used to repay war loans and assist previously great industrialists to pay back their own loans. Of course, this did not work. The circulation of paper money increased rapidly and soon Germans discovered that their money was worthless.

Paul and Herta (Papa and Mutti) arrived to find a city in turmoil, a place utterly alien to them in so many ways. But, having got there, with hope in their hearts, they hugged one another in reassurance and considered how on earth they would manage to make their way to the address they had for Herr Schneider. They had absolutely no idea whatsoever in which direction they should go. Despite all the conversations they had with tourists before the war about the size of Berlin they had not been able to fully comprehend how extensive a city it was. The place was mind-boggling.

Finally, they decided to ask for help at an information stand. As luck would have it, the clerk was ready to lend a hand and explained that it was probably too far for them to walk but they could take a tram and further explained where they needed to go to get the tram. Once the correct tram was located and they got on, they set off on their way towards the district of Charlottenburg. They proceeded in utter awe, staring out of the window of the tram, mesmerised by all saw. Never had they ever seen the like before. It was only a short journey and it was not long before they had reached their destination.

Alighting from the tram, they asked for directions from a passer-by and quickly located the house. As they stood outside and looked up at the property, they could not quite take in what they saw and gasped in utter astonishment. The house was massive, a mansion, a stunning property with the most magnificent architecture. Gingerly grasping the elaborate wrought iron gates, they peered through, their eyes following the sweeping drive to the house which had a splendid double-fronted door and then, still totally in awe, in unison, their heads titled back as they looked upwards to the uppermost point of the house which was several stories high.

There were extensive gardens to the front with an enormous fountain spurting out water in the most intricate fashion through the mouths of what appeared to be huge fishes. The gardens encircled the house and were far more extensive to the rear. It was then that a deep apprehension enveloped them both. They had no idea whatsoever that the Schneiders lived in such opulence or even, for that matter, if they lived in the house at all. What were they to do? Again, as always, Papa took command of the situation. They had not travelled all this way to be knocked back at the first hurdle. They had the invitation and so they would go up the drive, knock on the front door and ask to speak to Herr. Schneider. If they were turned away, then so be it, but they must at least make the effort.

With great trepidation, they opened a side gate and tentatively started to walk up the drive. Papa then, with the bit between his teeth, began to walk faster and faster, Mutti finally having to run to keep up. They arrived at the double-fronted door. Taking a few deep breaths, Papa pulled the bell. After what seemed an eternity, the door opened. They half expected a servant to face them but instead, it was Herr Schneider himself. At first, he stared at them and then after only a few seconds, realised who they were and greeted them in a most incredibly warm and friendly manner. He was genuinely utterly delighted to see them and could not quite believe they had made their way to him from Oderberg. He immediately ushered them into the drawing room where Frau Schneider was sitting working on a tapestry. Again, as soon as she saw them and realised who they were, they received an identical reception. They could not have hoped to have been so warmly greeted.

Within a few days Herr Schneider, knowing that Papa had butchery experience, arranged for him to take up a position at the main slaughterhouse near to Alexanderplatz. Herta was given work as a housemaid as they had no choice but to explain that she was pregnant, and therefore Frau Schneider thought it more sensible for Mutti to work in the house and do what she could, rather than going out of the house to work. But, although they were extremely appreciative of all the Schneiders had done for them, Papa felt it better that, as soon as they could, they should find themselves a small apartment to bring up his family. Once again Herr Schneider, through his contacts, found a small apartment in Zechliner Straße, in the Pankow District of Berlin. It only had a small bedroom, a living room/cum kitchenette and a washroom. But the rent was manageable, and it was within a reasonable distance from the slaughterhouse.

All too soon in some ways, they left the Schneider's luxurious home and settled swiftly into their new home, awaiting the arrival of their firstborn. The furniture was sparse but then again, so was the apartment and little was needed. They had the essentials: the apartment was new, had running water and an inside toilet and that was as much as they could ask for. Frau Schneider had given them a trunk full of household goods to start them off, which included linens, crockery, cutlery, pots and pans. She had also included a few items of bric-a-brac to brighten up the place. And, to their astonishment, on the day they moved in, a bed, table, chairs, stove, cot and a box of children's clothes arrived. They would always be indebted to the Schneiders and could not comprehend why they were so incredibly generous to a young couple that they basically only briefly knew. Perhaps it was because they had no children of their own.

What my parents did not know at the time was that the Schneiders were Jewish. Although there was some anti-Semitism around, nothing could predict what was to come only a few years in the distance. The Schneiders did not outwardly show that they were Jews. There was nothing in their house that my parents could remember that indicated that they were either. Perhaps the

Schneiders had an inkling of what was to come, and so chose to hide their religion. Sadly, they were never to know.

Chapter 3

I finally arrived on the 20th of February 1920, and they named me Erika Charlotte (after the Queen consort Sophia Charlotte and the district that the Schneider's lived) Hildegard. I no longer have my birth certificate. No idea what happened to it but somewhere over the years, it has been lost. But I do have my baptism certificate.

Baptism certificate 25th February 1923

It was into economical and constitutional chaos that I had put in my appearance. Life for most Germans was not easy, and my parents were no exception. They had few personal possessions and the flat in the tenement block was tiny. Although they both did the best they could to provide the barest of essentials, it was incredibly hard.

The slaughterhouse Papa worked in was a dreadful place. He worked long hours, leaving home at 5 am and not getting back until nightfall. Sanitation was appalling, as was safety. Our situation was hard, but the love between my parents sustained us. We had nothing but, in turn, wanted for nothing. Papa would come home utterly exhausted, but still find time to play with me.

When I was around six months old, Mutti managed to get a cleaning job and I was looked after by Frau Braun, one of the neighbours. She already had three children to look after so another one was not a problem. Money was incredibly tight but if ever Papa was able to bring some meat home, he always gave a portion to the Brauns.

On 1st September 1922 my brother, Gerhard Walter Schild, was born. Again, it was a happy event and our family seemed complete. He was a happy child and not a problem at all. It was lovely for me to have a little brother to play with. Mutti gave up her cleaning job now that she had two children to look after. Money was always tight and so our lives were not easy, to say the least. But I had a happy childhood. However, our continued happiness was not to be.

The first tragedy to violently hit us was the untimely death of my brother. At the tender age of only six, my dear brother died. He contracted pneumonia and despite every effort, he could not be saved. It seemed so very unfair. He was a sweet, happy little boy, taken all too soon. Tragedy then struck us again.

The second tragedy occurred only two years after dear Gerhard was taken. Late one afternoon in November 1930, there was a knock on the door. It was a policeman. He came to tell Mutti that there has been an accident at the slaughterhouse and Papa had been severely injured. He had been taken to the local hospital, but it was unlikely that he would survive. Mutti was utterly distraught. She left me with Frau Braun and went straight to the hospital. But quite quickly, she was back home again. Her beloved Paul had gone. He was only 42 years old. She was left with me to look after. She again would need to get work as a cleaner and the extremely meagre wages would have to sustain us. Papa was buried on 20th November 1930 at the cemetery in Stephanus, Berlin-Wedding alongside my brother.

Mutti was, once more, utterly devastated and found it so hard to reconcile the fact that two of those nearest to her had been taken away all too soon. She had the unenviable task of sending another telegram to the family in Oderberg with the dreadful news. The response was for her to immediately return home to the family, but this was not what she intended to do. No matter what future disasters should befall us, she was resolutely determined to continue to follow my papa's wishes and to make a life for the two of us in Berlin.

I suppose it was my parent's upbringing that enabled them to cope with any predicament. Despite being distressed and feeling totally alone, she was determined to manage. Papa's wish was for a better life for them in Berlin and although she could have packed up and taken me back to her family in Oderberg, who undoubtedly would have welcomed us with opened arms, she wanted to carry on with what Papa had visualised. She therefore came to an amicable arrangement with Frau Braun to look after me, and she would take on other jobs to make ends meet. And with the fortitude that she always showed throughout her life, she did precisely that.

Erika Schild January 1938 – aged 8

As previously mentioned, following the end of WW1, The Weimar Republic was formed as Germany's government. This was as a result of a national assembly after Kaiser Wilhelm II abdicated on 9th November 1918. The name came from the town of Weimar where the assembly was held. Several years of utter desolation followed the end of WW1 with many Germans feeling a complete sense of hopelessness. With the economy in ruins, most savings for the rich having been wiped out, and utter despair being the norm, the only way that the populous could get out of the doldrums was to instead be upbeat. This seething pressure by the masses to change their lives led to a period of despair intertwined with hyper festivity, resulting in what would later be referred to as 'the golden age' of prosperity for the city. Berlin was beginning to change drastically.

The early 1920s was a vibrant period in the history of Berlin and the austerity immediately after the end of WW1 was fading into a distant memory. Berlin became a haven for Bohemians. Many artists, writers, actors, filmmakers and the like, came to the city, as did those connected with science and philosophy. Berlin quickly became a city of extremes. Nothing was unexpected.

But, brewing behind this decade of decadence was the formation of what was to, once again, become the downfall of a nation.

The German Workers Party was a short-lived political party established in Weimar Germany after WW1. It was the precursor of the Nazi Party. The GWP (DAP in German) only lasted from 5th January 1919 until 24th February 1920. It then became the National Socialist German Workers Party – The Nazi Party.

In 1919, a young man, Adolf Hitler, joined their ranks and quickly gained recognition.

Adolf Hitler was born in Austria, then part of Austria-Hungary and was raised near Linz. He moved to Germany in 1913, and was decorated during his service in the German Army in World War I.

He was appointed leader of the Nazi Party in July 1921. In November 1923, Hitler had decided that the time was right for an attempt to seize power in Munich, in the hope that the Reichswehr (the post-war German military) would mutiny against the Berlin government and join his revolt.

On the night of 8 November, the Nazis used a patriotic rally in a Munich beer hall to launch an attempted *putsch* ('coup d'état'). This so-called Beer Hall Putsch attempt failed almost at once when the local *Reichswehr* commanders refused to support it. On the morning of 9 November, the Nazis staged a march of about 2,000 supporters through Munich in an attempt to rally support. Troops opened fire and 16 Nazis were killed. Hitler, Ludendorff and a number of others were arrested and were tried for treason in March 1924. They were given lenient prison sentences.

In jail, Hitler dictated the first volume of his autobiography and political manifesto *Mein Kampf* ('My Struggle').

After his release in 1924, Hitler gained popular support by attacking the Treaty of Versailles and promoting Pan-Germanism, anti-Semitism and anti-communism with charismatic oratory and Nazi propaganda. He frequently denounced international capitalism and communism as part of a Jewish conspiracy.

Adolf Hitler is a name which, when mentioned, brings shame to many Germans and is, and will forever be, directly associated with, and responsible for, the massacre of millions of innocent people, mainly Jews, or the disabled or those who did not fit in with his wish of a totally Aryan perfect society for Germany.

But, at the beginning of his rise through the political ranks, the main objective was to make Germany a great nation again. He was an incredible orator and motivated those he spoke to. He gave the nation back its pride in itself and convincing them that they could be great again. I suppose in a sense, he was able to brainwash the whole nation. His increase in popularity was at such a great pace and quite astonishing.

Between 1924 and 1929, The Weimar Republic managed to get hyperinflation under control. However, in order to do so, millions were borrowed from overseas, primarily America. When Wall Street crashed in 1929, America demanded their loans repaid and Germany was effectively left bankrupt again. It was at this time, unbeknown to the simple man on the street, that Germany was about to embark on its most horrifying period of history and Hitler played the continuing unsettled times to his advantage. Unemployment increased year on year from 1930.

The Weimar Republic was on the wane.

Hitler continued to speak at rallies to motivate the populous. Hundreds of thousands came to listen to him. It was inevitable that he would at some point be appointed chancellor, and that fateful day finally occurred on 30th January 1933.

Hitler was determined to expand industrial production and to bring about a massive infrastructure-improvement campaign. This resulted in unemployment being significantly reduced as labour was required to build numerous dams, autobahns, railroads and civil buildings. Following a recommendation, Joseph Goebbels (soon to be propaganda minister) commissioned a young architect, Albert Speer, to renovate the Party's headquarters in Berlin. When the project concluded, Speer returned to his home in Mannheim. However, the following year he was again requested by Goebbels to handle further renovations, this time to his ministry building on Wilhelmplatz.

This was to be the beginning of a long and fruitful employment for Speer. Following several smaller projects, he finally came to be noticed by Hitler and was unexpectedly invited for lunch. Hitler explained his vision to Speer and wanted him to be responsible to realise his dream of an architecturally supreme Germany. They became close friends during this period and Speer quickly became part of Hitler's inner circle.

The speed that Speer worked was astonishing. New building projects were appearing all over Germany but predominantly in Berlin, where Hitler's vision was systematically being implemented.

Hitler firmly believed in family values and that children were important for the nation and education should play a key role in the formation of Nazi Germany. Mind you, there was an ulterior motive for this – I do not think Hitler did anything without a warped notion of what could be achieved. Enhancing education was primarily to allow those in power to be in a position of being able to indoctrinate children, through schooling, into becoming loyal Nazis by the time they reached adulthood.

Outside school, the Hitler Youth Organisation became a dominant part of German culture and all other youth groups were abolished. When Hitler became chancellor in 1933, membership was 100k. Some three years later in 1936, it was nearer to 4 million.

It was during this period of great change, at the start of Hitler being chancellor, that I, a child of 13 years old, was personally, and unexpectedly, to benefit.

Chapter 4

With no Papa, and Mutti earning little, in the old republic there would have been no opportunity for me to attend a gymnasium (grammar school). But, under Nazi Germany, I was selected and given a grant to attend one. Why I was chosen, I am afraid I do not know. I had no idea at the time how significant this act by the state would prove to be for me.

I was so excited. My parents, although only with a basic education, were by no means stupid. They were both shrewd, with an abundance of common sense together with an extraordinary ability, or sixth sense, to know what to do for the best. They would never have been led down a path not of their choosing. For me to go to a grammar school meant I would have the opportunity of an excellent education. If I worked hard and attained good qualifications, when I left school I might be in a better situation to acquire a good job and perhaps be able to financially help Mutti. But this was all in the future.

At the time, of course, I had no idea what the implications were concerning all the significant and astonishing changes that were gradually coming into force throughout Germany in the 1930s. I was a youngster and blindly accepted everything that I was told without question. I have no recollection of Mutti making any derogatory remarks about the sweeping transformations that were occurring. Whether she had any views at the time I cannot say. Years later, when I asked her, she always flatly refused to discuss it.

A foreigner will certainly find it totally unfathomable to understand how virtually a whole nation could be so indoctrinated and basically brainwashed, but that is precisely how it was. Maybe it was because of the deep despair which virtually every German felt during the time before Hitler, so when he came into power he gave Germans a sense of purpose and hope, I do not know. It would be nearly two decades later when I would finally leave Germany, utterly ashamed of all that had happened in the preceding years. Mutti's choice of not discussing anything that happened in Germany during the 1930s and 1940s is what I can now fully understand as I too felt the same. It is with a heavy heart that I recall certain events that I directly witnessed.

Those appalling images and memories are still with me today. However, in order to illustrate my upbringing, it is essential that I recall as much as I can. But I am getting ahead of myself.

The whole school curriculum changed in 1933. Education was to play an important part in the propaganda of the nation. It was envisaged that by making sweeping changes, it would cultivate a loyal following of Hitler, the Nazi party and their vision for the country. The Hitler Youth was initiated, and this was a further way of creating loyal Nazis by the time they reached adulthood.

Of course, by making such drastic changes to the curriculum, it was quite dependant on the teachers delivering the message. All teachers were vetted by a local member of the Nazi party and, if they were considered disloyal, they were immediately dismissed. For those remaining to be fully conversant with the new curriculum, many attended lessons during the school holidays where the details of the new learning processes were made abundantly clear. It was essential that teachers were careful not to be disparaging about the new agenda in front of the children, as the children were encouraged to report any dissent and again, anyone deemed to be not fully compliant, were dismissed.

All subjects were to change but it was history and biology which were the most significantly affected. The teaching of history was based on the glorification of Germany and a nationalist approach was compulsory. Significant German historical events which could be defined as not showing Germany in a good light, such as the uprisings in 1918, were 'massaged' and explained as being the fault of infiltration from Jews and Marxists, and the hyperinflation in 1923 was blamed on Jewish saboteurs. The propaganda machine was at work and, little by little, it soon became all too evident that all the problems that Germany faced were to be blamed on the Jews.

This was apparent in the new approach to teaching biology. The subject became predominately the study of different races to prove the Nazi philosophy that they were racially superior. This programming began when children were only six years old. Hitler stated that all children should leave school with the knowledge of the necessity and meaning of blood purity. It was drummed into the children that they must be selective when choosing a partner, marrying, and having children of their own. Inter-racial marriages were utterly outlawed, and children were taught that to do so would result in a rapid decline in racial purity.

The other noteworthy change was physical education. This became an important part of the curriculum and accounted for 15% of the weekly timetable. Boxing was compulsory for boys, and they were expected to suffer pain in order to become tough young men. The children received regular fitness tests and any found lacking could be expelled. Should this occur, they would face incredible humiliation. Consequently, children pushed themselves much harder to avoid disgrace.

There were differences between the education of boys and girls. At the age of 12, any boy who was considered 'special' and physically fitter and stronger than the rest was sent to one of the Adolf Hitler Schools. It was incredibly tough for these children and they endured years of physical training and instruction. Classes began each morning at 7 am and included studies in philosophy, politics and world history. Afternoons were devoted to military drills, battle tactics, sports and equestrian techniques. When they reached 18 years of age, they either left for university or went straight into the army. At this stage, there was yet further selection.

Those deemed as being the best were sent to the most elite of all schools, the Order Castles. Here the boys were further nurtured with yet more rigorous training and indoctrination. They were driven to extreme physical endurance. War games, often using live ammunition were a regular occurrence. Those who managed to survive this intense training were expected, when leaving the school, to attain a high-ranking position in the army or SS (Shultzstaffell formed in 1925 by Hitler as a group of personal bodyguards which grew to over 250,000 troops by 1939).

For girls, it was completely different, though they too received programming of sorts. Hitler made it abundantly clear what he perceived the role of women in Germany to be. They should dedicate their lives to being good mothers and bringing up children, remaining in the home whilst their husbands worked. Although there were certain specialist areas that women could work in, he firmly believed that there was no reason why women should work.

From their early years, girls were taught that to be a good German woman required them to marry at a young age, keep a decent home for her husband and to have many children. With Hitler in power, one of the first acts that was passed was the Law of the Encouragement of Marriage. This law stated that all newly married couples would get a government loan of 1,000 Marks, which was equivalent to approximately nine months of income.

Obviously, this was an incredibly generous proposal that resulted in roughly 800,000 couples immediately taking up the offer. It was made more inviting as it did not have to be repaid in a normal way; instead, on the birth of the first child, 25% of the loan was written off, two children meant 50% and four children meant the entire loan was cleared. The aim of the law was simply to encourage newlyweds to have as many children as they could. But this law was passed with disturbing intentions. It was solely a way of propagating more children into the Fatherland who could be programmed in the philosophies of the Nazi party.

Hitler already had a vision of world domination and to do that, he needed loyal supporters. What better way than to have numerous children who, from an early age, are systematically brainwashed into following his aspirations, without question. Despite this indoctrination, girls were also given the opportunity of an excellent formal education.

As I mentioned earlier, I was selected to attend a grammar school. I was not the archetypal Aryan blue-eyed blonde. My hair and eyes were dark, but I had a good physical appearance and was deemed as being quite pretty. Again, as I was only 12 years old, I had no real knowledge or understanding as to why I was selected for a grammar school, but I was. I know my Mutti was immensely proud as no one in the family before me had received such an opportunity. Knowing how much a good education meant, I was determined to work hard and make sure that I learned as much as possible. As well as the core subjects, we were also taught needlework, sewing and knitting; things I excelled at. I especially enjoyed sewing.

When I was 13, Mutti was able to obtain an old second-hand sewing machine from a neighbour, that was no longer wanted, and she did not have to pay for it in cash – just a few hours of spring-cleaning sufficed. Of course, my utter enthusiasm for this extremely womanly task was highly commended by my teachers, as it was totally in keeping with the Nazi philosophy for women in the Third Reich.

No one in my immediate family or friends or neighbours had much money, and so it was with great joy that I was able to help in a little way. I would collect unwanted clothing from here, there, and everywhere. I would then carefully unpick it all. With the remnants I ended up with, I would make new clothes and sell them for a few Marks. I rapidly gained a reputation in the local neighbourhood and anyone who needed alterations, or a cheap outfit, would come to me.

Of course, I also benefitted. I was gradually able to gain a wardrobe full of lovely clothes; all of which had been produced for virtually nothing and I quickly became the envy of all my friends. However, it was when I went out that my skills truly showed their potential. Invariably, everyone would remark about how beautiful and well-dressed I looked – and me being only a schoolgirl.

The joy I had for needlework remained with me all my life and this skill helped me greatly on more than one occasion.

Chapter 5

The next important event for me and Mutti was my confirmation. Mutti was a devout Lutheran and it was particularly important for her that I should be baptised and confirmed. I have to say I was not as enthusiastic as Mutti to regularly attend services, but I did not object to her wishes.

Confirmation certificate 4th March 1934

Erika Schild on day of confirmation aged 14

Considering the events which would happen a few years from now, it was ironic in some ways that English was taught. It became one of my favourite subjects and something I seemed to be able to learn with ease and showed a real aptitude for. I was, therefore, placed in a special class specifically for those children who showed great promise. It was considered to be complementary to our education to learn more about America and to improve our written English. Not long after my confirmation day, the children in my class were selected to have a pen friend to write to in America. The girl that I was given to correspond with was Marietta Meyer. She was two years younger than me and lived in Detroit Lakes, Minnesota. Her parents were Phillip (PJ) and Etta Meyer.

It was extremely exciting for me to correspond with someone so far away on the other side of the world. What I didn't know at the time was that this friendship would last a lifetime and, without doubt, the Meyer family would become one of the most important aspects of my life and a friendship that I am forever eternally grateful for, with all my heart.

As a teenager, I and my close friends had little understanding or appreciation of the political facets of Germany. We all followed like sheep, blindly accepted everything we were being told, and never questioned anything. The propaganda machine was driving at a phenomenal pace and we were all being suckered in hook, line and sinker. At school, I had three close friends: two sisters, Inge (Ingeborg) and Ushi (Ursula) together with Ellie (Eleanor). We spent hours and hours together; gossiping, going to the pictures and dreaming about what we would achieve and where our lives would take us. But the one thing we all absolutely adored was meeting boys and going dancing. This was all too easy for us during the late 1930s. I don't think we could have been in a better place to play out our fantasies.

Berlin was a city of extremes with so much to see and do. During the 1920s and 1930s, Berlin saw huge changes. The city became a mecca for every conceivable vice. Cabaret was synonymous with Berlin and nowhere else in the world was it done better. When Hitler became chancellor, the city was growing and growing, with new buildings cropping up all over the place. Wilhelm Straße saw many new buildings built, at a colossal pace, all to accommodate the growing Nazi party and all the newly formed ministries.

School certificate from 1935

Of course, one other significant building project was for the 1936 Olympics. Although the Olympics for 1936 had been given to Germany, it was done so before Hitler came into power. It did, however, give him the perfect platform to demonstrate to the world how efficient Nazi Germany was. The Nazi belief that they were unconquerable was in full view during the games. The athletes of the

German team were pushed to their limits, training full time for what was an amateur competition. But they wanted to prove they were the master race.

However, all was not going to go their way. They had not foreseen that an African American, Jesse Owens, would dominate the games. He won four gold medals but, under Nazi ideology, he was racially inferior.

During the games, Goebbels and his propaganda ministry were in full flow. The Nazi Party wanted to be seen in the best light and, therefore, decided to hide the phenomenal number of anti-Semitic posters which were now prevalent all-around Berlin. Anything which portrayed these sentiments such as 'Jews not welcome' were removed or hidden. Everyone was expected to be seen as happy-go-lucky, all living and working together in harmony with the ultimate aim of ensuring the world saw a united Germany, thus ensuring that the games ran effortlessly. Of course, it was all a total farce. Within a few years, Hitler, in pursuit of dominance over Europe, would once more take Germany to war.

Chapter 6

When it was time for me to leave school, in May 1935, I considered several options. Dressmaking was particularly important to me, but I did not feel it would be the way for me to earn a living. My education was good and so I felt that I should look for employment in a business, where there was a chance of promotion. I was 15 when I left school, and decided upon secretarial work of some kind.

My spoken and written English was excellent, and I thought that it may come in use at some point. It was important for me to continue to learn in order to be able to attain a good position, as I wanted to make the most of the excellent education I had received. I needed to think of my mother and financially help her. We were still living in the same flat and although it was tough on us, we did manage to have a reasonable standard of living.

I enrolled with C Jessen-Axster on Pestalozzi Straße 37, Berlin-Pankow, for typing and shorthand lessons. This was from May 1935 until March 1936. When I left, I was typing at 150 words a minute.

Reference from C Jessen-Axster

On 1st April 1936, I started my first job working for a dentist, Dr Karl Printz on Flora Straße 90, Berlin-Pankow. This was a big step for me. I was only 16 years old and earning my first wage – which was not much at all. I acted as the receptionist, kept records, assisted him when he was with patients, cleaned instruments and handled any correspondence. My ambition finally got the better of me and, in early 1938, I started looking for another position.

Reference from Dr Karl Prinz

Also, around the same time, Mutti and I moved to a new apartment on Kolonie Straße 43, Berlin-Gesundbrunnen. I applied for a few roles and finally was accepted as a personal assistant to a patent lawyer, Dr Arthur Ullrich on Rüdesheimer Platz 10, Berlin-Wilmersdorf. This was the most perfect job. Dr Ullrich was an incredibly kind and thoughtful man. I started with him on 1st May 1938.

The Nazis were growing stronger and stronger, as was their indoctrination of the people of Germany, together with the offensive of eradicating all those of the Jewish faith. Their anti-Semitism stance was being cultivated at a phenomenal pace. I have to say, when I think back to these times, I too had fallen under the spell being cast. We truly believed that what Hitler was trying to achieve for Germany was in the country's best interests to make the nation a global power. We simply did not question the philosophy.

On 7th November 1938, a German embassy official in Paris was assassinated by the disaffected Polish Jew, Herschel Grynszpan. This act was the catalyst for the Nazis to systematically begin the annihilation of Jews.

On 9th November 1938, Kristallnacht occurred. Also called the November Pogrom, it was the persecution against Jews carried out by SA paramilitary forces and civilians throughout Nazi Germany. The German authorities looked on without intervening. The name Kristallnacht comes from the shards of broken glass that littered the streets after the windows of Jewish-owned stores, buildings and synagogues were smashed.

Jewish homes, hospitals and schools were ransacked as the attackers demolished buildings with sledgehammers. The rioters destroyed 267 synagogues throughout Germany, Austria and the Sudetenland. Over 7,000 Jewish businesses were damaged or destroyed, and 30,000 Jewish men were arrested and incarcerated in concentration camps. British historian, Martin Gilbert, wrote that no event in the history of German Jews between 1933 and 1945 was so widely reported as it was happening, and the accounts from foreign journalists working in Germany sent shockwaves around the world.

The Times of London observed on 11th November 1938: 'No foreign propagandist bent upon blackening Germany before the world could outdo the tale of burnings and beatings, of blackguardly assaults on defenceless and innocent people, which disgraced that country yesterday.'

Early reports estimated that 91 Jews had been murdered. Modern analysis of German scholarly sources puts the figure much higher; when deaths from post-arrest maltreatment and subsequent suicides are included, the death toll climbs into the hundreds, with Richard J. Evans estimating 638 suicide deaths. Historians view Kristallnacht as a prelude to the final solution and the murder of six million Jews during the Holocaust.

Of the fourteen synagogues in Berlin at the time, eleven were burnt down completely, and the other three were badly damaged. Over 1,000 Jews were arrested and deported to Sachsenhausen concentration camp which was located 19 miles northwest of Berlin in Oranienburg. Tens of thousands eventually died there.

In 1933, there were around 160,000 Jews in Berlin: one-third of all Jews in Germany and 4% of the Berlin population. Many were poor immigrants from Eastern Europe, and they lived mainly around Alexanderplatz.

Following Kristallnacht, this reduced to around 75,000. This single event is often referred to as the beginning of the holocaust. The nature of the Nazi persecution of the Jews was changing from economic, political and social to physical, with beatings, incarceration and murder.

Following this horrendous night, our dear friends, the Schneiders, thankfully realised that staying in Berlin was far too much of a risk. They were already being targeted because of their wealth, and were akin to prisoners in their own home. So, reluctantly, they decided that they needed to leave. Not just Berlin, but Germany. Quickly they sold up, not achieving the true value of their property. But they took what they could and emigrated to the USA. They lived the remainder of their lives in comfort away from the horrors to come for so many of their faith, never returning to Germany.

At a conference on the day after Kristallnacht, Hermann Göring said: "The Jewish problem will reach its solution if, in anytime soon, we will be drawn into war beyond our border. Then it is obvious that we will have to manage a final account with the Jews." Kristallnacht was also instrumental in changing global opinion. In the United States, for instance, it was this specific incident that came to symbolise Nazism and was the reason the Nazis became associated with evil.

In August 1939, my mother moved from our flat in Kolonie Straße into an apartment on her own on Schöneweider Straße, Berlin, Neukölln. This was to be her home for the rest of her days. It was again a small apartment, on the first floor of a block but, as she was on her own, it was all that was needed.

On 1st September 1939, Germany invaded Poland. Two days later, on 3rd September 1939, Neville Chamberlain, the UK Prime Minister, gave his speech in declaration of war by France and the United Kingdom. His speech is as follows:

I am speaking to you from the Cabinet Room at 10, Downing Street. This morning the British ambassador in Berlin handed the German government a final note stating that unless we heard from them by 11 o'clock, that they were prepared at once to withdraw their troops from Poland, a state of war would exist between us. I have to tell you now that no such undertaking has been received, and that consequently, this country is at war with Germany.

You can imagine what a bitter blow it is to me that all my long struggle to win peace has failed. Yet I cannot believe that there is anything more or anything different that I could have done and that would have been more successful. Up to the very last, it would have been quite possible to have arranged a peaceful and honourable settlement between Germany and Poland, but Hitler would not have it. He had evidently made up his mind to attack Poland whatever happened, and although he now says he put forward reasonable proposals which were rejected by the Poles, that is not a true statement.

The proposals were never shown to the Poles nor to us, and though they were announced in a German broadcast on Thursday night, Hitler did not wait to hear comments on them, but ordered his troops to cross the Polish frontier the next morning. His action shows convincingly that there is no chance of expecting that this man will ever give up his practice of using force to gain his will. He can only be stopped by force, and we and France are today, in fulfilment of our obligations, going to the aid of Poland, who is so bravely resisting this wicked and unprovoked attack upon her people.

We have a clear conscience. We have done all that any country could do to establish peace. The situation in which no word given by Germany's ruler could be trusted and no people or country could feel safe has become intolerable. And now that we have resolved to finish it, I know that you will all play your part with calmness and courage. At such a moment as this, the assurances of support which we have received from the Empire are a source of profound encouragement to us. When I have finished speaking, certain detailed announcements will be made on behalf of the government. Give these your close attention.

The government has made plans under which it will be possible to carry on the work of the nation in the days of stress and strain that may be ahead. But these plans need your help. You may be taking your part in the fighting services or as a volunteer in one of the branches of civil defence. If so, you will report for duty in accordance with the instructions you receive.

You may be engaged in work essential to the prosecution of war for the maintenance of the life of the people – in factories, in transport, in public utility concerns or in the supply of other necessaries of life. If so, it is of vital importance that you should carry on with your jobs. Now may God bless you all and may He defend the right, for it is evil things that we shall be fighting against – brute force, bad faith, injustice, oppression and persecution – and against them I am certain that the right will prevail.

Life would never be the same again for millions of people. Not only in Europe but all over the world.

Chapter 7

Initially, at the outset of war, everyday life was not greatly affected. We all went about our daily routines. Hitler tried to keep rationing to a minimum as he knew that cutbacks during WW1 had led to political unrest, so he ordered that restrictions should be kept to a minimum. Unfortunately though, in December 1939, I was the recipient of bad news. Dr Ullrich, the patent lawyer I was working for, announced to me that he would have to let me go. Due to the start of the war, business for him slumped, and he had no choice but to give me notice.

Dr. Arthur Ullrich
Patentanwalt

Berlin-Wilmersdorf, den 30. Dezember 1939.
Rüdesheimer Platz 16

Zeugnis.

Fräulein Erika Schild, Berlin-Neukölln, Schöneweider Strasse 23, geboren am 17. Februar 1920, war vom 1. Mai 1936 bis 31. Dezember 1939 bei mir im Büro als Stenotypistin tätig. Sie war fleissig und pünktlich und hat während der ganzen Zeit kein einziges Mal gefehlt.

Fräulein Schild hat die ihr übertragenen Arbeiten mit grossem Fleiss und mit viel Interesse zu meiner vollsten Zufriedenheit ausgeführt. Sie stenographiert sehr flott und überträgt ihr Stenogramm in absolut einwandfreier Form in die Maschine. Bei den von ihr ausgeführten Arbeiten handelt es sich nicht nur um Briefe und Schriftstücke gewöhnlichen Inhalts, sondern auch um Schriftsätze, Gutachten usw., die wissenschaftlich komplizierte Fragen betreffen.

Zu meinem grossen Bedauern war ich im Hinblick auf den ganz allgemein bei der Anwaltschaft herrschenden Geschäftsrückgang gezwungen, Fräulein Schild zu kündigen.

Reference from Dr Arthur Ullrich

Thankfully though, almost immediately, I was able to find another job and, on 2nd January 1940, I started with Gesellschaft Für Luftfahrtbedarf. They were manufacturers of aircraft parts.

Following the invasion of France, in June 1940, consumer goods began to flow into Germany which helped to reduce shortages. Berlin was at the extreme range of British bombers. However, on 7th June 1940, the first allied bomber attacked Berlin. Eight bombs were dropped. Hitler immediately retaliated and ordered a counter strike on the United Kingdom and the blitz commenced.

We tried to manage day to day, and continue with our lives, but it was not easy. Several male friends had joined the armed forces and I knew that, in most cases, I would probably not see them again. One friend was Wilhelm Müller. We had met before the war whilst I was working for Dr Karl Printz. Wilhelm was a client of the dentist. Wilhelm was the son of an industrialist and from quite a wealthy family. He had a series of appointments and during this time we got to know one another and then had a few dates, though nothing serious.

My background was from a relatively poor environment. Although I had a good education, I was somewhat lacking in social skills. Though I did not perhaps realise to what extent.

In May 1940, Wilhelm met me for a drink and to let me know that he would be soon leaving to join the army. He said he wanted me to meet his family. I was not sure about this at all, but he was insistent. Of course, I knew I could dress smartly as I had an extensive array of dresses, but I knew his family were 'posh' and I was apprehensive about meeting them. But Willi insisted and said I should not worry – his family were down to earth, and they would love me.

So, the date was arranged for me to have afternoon tea with them at their house in Grunewald. Willi came to me to pick me up and we drove to his home. They lived in an exclusive part of Berlin and you had to have money to buy a property in this district. It did not take long to get there and, when we pulled up outside, I was most impressed with the house. It was large and double fronted with extensive gardens.

Everyone was extremely pleasant towards me and I was made to feel at ease. All was going well until…following a formal afternoon tea, I was given an orange, on a plate with a knife. I had absolutely no idea that there was a certain way that oranges should be eaten. For me, the easiest way was to stick my thumb nail into the top and then start to peel it. As I was doing this, I suddenly became aware that everyone was watching me, and I had no idea why. Willi leant over and quietly whispered to me that I should have used the knife to peel the orange. I was mortified. I had tried so hard to make an impression and had failed abysmally.

Kindly, Willi realising how embarrassed I was, made our excuses and we left.

This event had a profound effect on me. The following morning, I went to a bookshop and bought a book on etiquette. I studied this book from cover to cover and followed the instructions from that day to this. Over the years, family and friends have laughed at me for being so particular with manners, but I take no notice. I should also say that oranges were, and remain, a favourite fruit of mine. However, I only ever eat one using a plate and with a knife. It is a bit of a performance but regardless, I always go through the same process when preparing an orange to eat.

First, I make a circle at the top of the orange with a sharp knife and gradually lift off the lid. I then, again using the knife, make regularly spaced incisions around the whole orange from top to bottom. Each section is then carefully peeled back and removed. Any excess pith is removed and then the sections pulled apart and laid out on the plate. Only then, do I begin to eat them. To this day, I go through the routine each and every time I eat an orange.

Willem sadly died only weeks after joining up. Such a waste of a young life.

In the photo below I am wearing a brooch given to me by another dear friend, Helmut. It is a German Kreigsmarine MCO Boatswain insignia. Sadly, not long after this photo was taken, I received yet more awful news that Helmut had also been killed in action. Wilhelm and Helmut gone. So much sadness. Far too many people were being killed and many of my friends were no longer around. It all seemed so incredibly sad.

Erika Schild 22 September 1942

At the beginning of the war, the British targeted their bombing raids on industrial and military targets but, in 1942, the RAF switched to area bombing i.e., targeting large industrial cities with incendiary devices and not distinguishing between military and civilian. However, during 1942, Berlin had some respite as the bombing campaign stopped. We were being lulled into a false sense of security. As the Nazi government was based in Berlin, we knew in our hearts that it was only a matter of time before the Allies starting bombing again.

As expected, in March 1943, it started again and the bombing became more regular and devastating. With all the bombing and rationing, life in Berlin was becoming extremely difficult. Huge shelters had been built which could hold around 65,000 people. Nevertheless, eventually, Berliners began to flee the city as life was quickly becoming impossible.

Much had been written about the horrors of war. I will not go into too many details as the purpose of this narrative is to bring the events of my younger life to the point of my story which is meeting my one and only true love, my dearest darling John.

Following the devastating bombing attack in March 1943, I unexpectedly received a letter from Dr Ullrich. He had decided to move his practice out of Berlin. It was simply not possible to run the business from there any longer as life had become intolerable. He asked if I would be willing to leave Berlin and once again be his secretary at his new offices.

This was a huge decision to make but I thought why not. He was a nice and kind man. I discussed it with Mutti, and she agreed I should go. I suppose she also thought that it would be safer for me away from Berlin. It would take a couple of months to get organised and prepare to relocate.

In July 1942, I gave in my notice to my current employers. Gesellschaft Für Luftfahrtbedarf. I was soon to be off on another journey of my life.

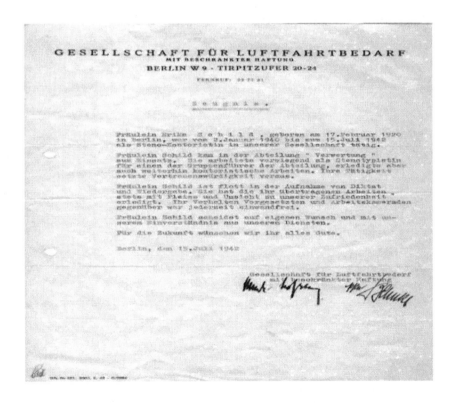

Reference from Gesellschaft Für Luftfahrtbedarf

Our destination was to the southeast of Germany and a small town called Hirschberg Riesengebirge in lower Silesia close to the border with Poland. Our business address here was Herman Goring Straße 17, which as with all streets that had been given this name during WW2, at the end of WW2, they were all changed. As it happens, this town area used to be part of Poland but became part of the German Empire in 1871. It reverted again to Poland following the Potsdam Conference in 1945 and is now known as Jelenia Góra.

Dr Ullrich had rented a house for himself and his family just outside the town and had arranged for me to rent a room in lodgings in the centre of town. He had arrived a few days before me to settle in his family and kindly met me at the station when I finally got there. He straight away took me to my lodgings and, on the way, showed me where the new office was and, thankfully, it was only a short walk away.

The first couple of weeks, I used my time getting the office organised whilst Dr Ullrich spent time communicating with his contacts and letting them know his business was up and running again.

Our lives here in this small town were relatively calm, though I often thought and worried about my mother, especially, and my friends who had remained in Berlin. Not a day would go by when I would not have them in my thoughts. We often had news of horrors occurring everywhere but at the time were utterly convinced that we were winning the war. We obviously heard stories of atrocities but truly believed that our fellow countrymen could not be party to these despicable events and it was the Allies rumourmongering.

In March 1944, Dr Ullrich was requested to make a declaration in relation to health insurance of my employment and earnings. This in itself is not interesting but as you can see from the copy of the letter, just above the signature it says Heil Hitler! This was a requirement for anything official and if you did not include it, you would invariably be targeted for a visit from the authorities.

z.Zt. (8) Hirschberg / Rsgb.,
Hermann-Göring-Strasse 17

31. März 1944

An die
Barmer Ersatzkasse
Geschäftsstelle Hirschberg

(8) Hirschberg / Rsgb.
Hermann-Göring-Strasse

Betr.: Fräulein Erika Schild - Mitglieds-Nr. 2 667 378

Ich habe mein Büro von Berlin-Wilmersdorf, Künesheimer Platz 10, teilverlegt nach Hirschberg, Hermann-Göring-Strasse 17. Meine Stenotypistin Fräulein Erika Schild, die bisher in Berlin-Pankow, Parkstrasse 12b wohnte, ist jetzt in Hirschberg, Lichte Burgstrasse 2 ansässig. Ihr Gehalt erhöht sich mit Wirkung vom 1. April 1944 auf RM 270,-- (erstmalig am 30. April zur Auszahlung kommend). Hiervon werden RM 39,-- auf das Eiserne Sparkonto von Fräulein Schild abgeführt, so dass die Abzüge von RM 231,-- zu berechnen sind.

Heil Hitler !
gez. Dr. A. Ullrich

Confirmation of earnings for Erika Schild

Something that quickly brought home the reality of war was a postcard I received from a Berlin friend. He was serving in the German Army, had been captured and then sent to Canada into a prisoner of war camp. He was though, able to send me a postcard to let me know he was OK.

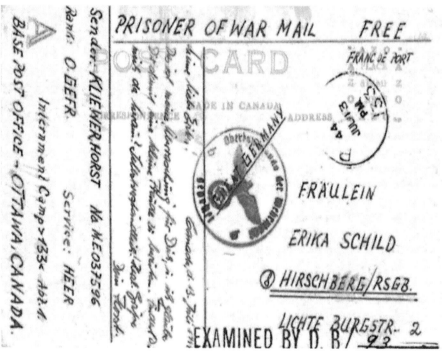

Post card from Horst Kliewer

This was the last communication I received from Horst; we lost touch with one another. I can only assume that no news was good news.

In August of 1944, we began to worry about our own safety. The Russians were advancing from the east at a rapid pace and Dr Ullrich felt that it was unsafe to remain where we were. He decided to relocate again, but this time to Heidelberg in the west of Germany. He could consider going back to Berlin, but we both knew that it had sustained severe damage, and also would be the focal point going forward for the Allies and Russians. To go back there and operate a business was not a possible option.

He had contacts in Heidelberg, and he felt for him, this was the best solution. For me though, this was unthinkable.

I needed to get back to Berlin, whatever the risk and whatever the state it was in. Darling Mutti was there and somehow, I had to get back there to check on her and try to persuade her to leave the city, though I knew in my heart that she was stubborn and would probably refuse to leave.

Whilst living in Hirschberg, I became friends with a local girl, Helga, who was an amateur photographer. She took a number of photos of me around this time.

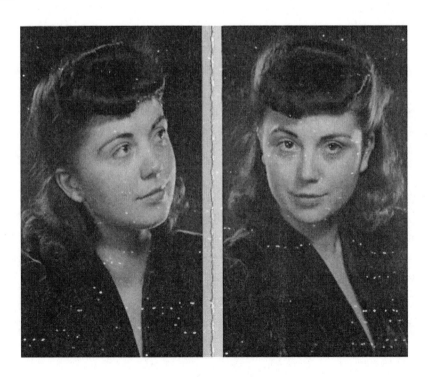

Erika Schild September 1944 – aged 24

Helga would give me instructions of how to pose for each photo, sometimes looking at the camera and other times away from it. Again, these instructions remained with me all my life and whenever having a photo taken, I will always pose making sure that I was standing correctly and even checking that my feet are placed properly.

Wanting to get to Berlin and actually making it there I knew would be fraught with difficulties. The transport infrastructure throughout much of Germany had now been decimated through bombing by the Allies.

At the start of the war Germany's transport system, comprising of modern autobahns, excellent railways and a complex network of interlinking canals and rivers were among the best in the world. But after autumn 1943, the connections between industrial centres became attractive bombing targets, which, when effectively bombed, badly affected the distribution of coal, which formed the basis of most military and industrial operations.

Soon large parts of Germany's remaining transport network were paralysed, and the Ruhr became economically isolated from the rest of the Reich. Ultimately it was the sustained Allied bombing of the transport network which broke Nazi resistance.

Despite incredible efforts at continually reorganising production after each setback, it was becoming nigh on impossible, and soon they would have to admit defeat in the armaments battle. German industry was now unable to keep up with the high number of 'Top Priority' weapons programs, such as the production of the V weapons and calls for 3,000 Me 262 jet fighters and bombers per month.

However, many factories were able to maintain production right up to the moment Allied forces arrived at the gates. By now the V1 and V2 launch sites were being increasingly overrun, and with the Allies moving towards the Rhine and the Soviet armies rapidly closing in from the east, large numbers of refugees began to congregate in the cities, creating utter chaos.

By the end of October 1944, Dr Ullrich and his family had left Hirschberg and moved on to Heidelberg and I was left alone. I knew I had to get out of the town as soon as possible before the Russians arrived.

We were now heading for winter and the weather forecast was not good. Severe frost and snow were expected in the New Year. In order to travel, I first had to apply for permission. It was not possible to move any distance in Germany without having official documentation and a plausible reason for making the journey. After a wait of a few weeks finally, on the 5th December 1944, I received my authorisation, and was able to start the trek to Berlin.

I knew this was not going to be a quick and easy slog, as many of the train lines and stations had been bombed and were impassable or simply no longer there, but I had to try. I started off the expedition by train with only a few possessions that I could manage to carry. For everything else I had no choice but to leave with my landlady to do with as she wanted.

Authorisation document December 1944

The first part of my journey was by train to Dresden. This part of the journey was actually without incident and quite easy. But, having arrived there, it soon quickly became apparent that the onward journey would not be so easy.

I was advised by station staff that getting to Berlin by train was impossible as there simply were no trains or train lines going north. I was distraught. I had no idea at what on earth I could do. I so wanted to get back to Berlin and see my dearest mutti.

I wandered around the station totally at a loss of what to do next.

Coffee – that is what was needed. I was absolutely parched and, by some miracle, I found a small café that was open near to the station. I sat down and was served my coffee. The coffee was weak, but it would do. I stared down into the cup hoping for some inspiration. I was feeling completely dejected. How on earth was I going to get back to Berlin and dearest Mutti. All of a sudden, a young man joined me at my table. I was somewhat taken aback by his eagerness to sit next to me and start chatting. But he seemed nice.

He told me his name was Erwin Gerath and that he had been invalided out of the German Army (though I could not see from his demeanour what the 'injury' could be). Anyway, he asked why I was looking so forlorn and I explained my situation and about needing to get back to Berlin. He immediately said he was my knight in shining armour as he had a solution for me.

To my complete surprise and utter amazement, he explained that he had a truck and fuel and was actually heading for Berlin himself and I was more than welcome to join him. This seemed astonishing and I could not believe my luck. Of course, I said yes. All I wanted was to get back to my mutti as quickly as possible.

He wanted to leave straight away so we set off almost instantly. We managed to grab a few provisions for the journey and then we were on our way. I knew that this decision of mine could be a great risk, to travel such a distance with a complete stranger but I felt I had no choice. I was obviously apprehensive and careful but there seemed to be no alternative.

Chapter 8

Although only around 190 km, we knew it would be a long and arduous journey which we expected to take several days: sleeping in the truck at night.

We saw so much wreckage on our journey. It certainly was truly heart-breaking.

Finally, on 13th December, we arrived in Berlin. First, we had to get past a traffic control post. Thankfully, we had the necessary authorisation so could prove who we were, where we had come from, and where we were going. It took a while but finally they stamped our documents and allowed us to continue our journey.

Erwin was the perfect gentleman throughout our trip. He carefully looked after me and showed no hint of bad behaviour whatsoever. He was an amusing travel companion and we spent much of our time chatting about family, the war, music and our lives to date. Strangely, he spoke little of his army life. But that did not overly concern me.

Having arrived, I was utterly shocked by the destruction and devastation. The Berlin that I knew and loved had gone. Many of the buildings that the Nazis had built so quickly after coming into power had been bombed. The Kaiser Wilhelm Memorial Church on Kurfürstendamm, which was a well-known location for me as not far from where I lived and worked, had been wrecked. Only part of the spire remained. It seemed futile. Was all this carnage worth it? A resounding no.

We drove on towards Neukölln. Tears streaming down my face as I looked around witnessing all the horror. Eventually, we managed to get to Schönweider Straße and Mutti. Incredibly, her building was still standing with virtually no damage. Mutti was overjoyed to see me. She could not quite believe that I was standing on her front doorstep. She hugged me as though she had not seen or heard from me in many years. Mutti was never particularly emotional or tactile so for her to react as she did was somewhat surprising.

Erwin dropped me off but did not come up to the flat with me to meet Mutti. He wanted to go off straight away and see if he could find his family. But he said he would pop back the following day to check in with me.

Mutti and I sat together for an age drinking coffee and catching up.

When I had left for Hirschberg, Mutti had given me some of her possessions for safe keeping to take with me. They were not of any monetary value, only sentimental. Understandably, when I explained to her that, as I had to leave Hirschberg quickly, I had no choice but to leave some of her possessions behind. She was of course quite upset. But, quickly realised that I had no choice and it was more important for me to have got back to her than her possessions.

Considering all that had gone on in Berlin, she appeared remarkably well. She was thinner, but then we all were. She had been able to manage, and the neighbours had been helping each other. She was stoic and matter of fact with all that was going on. This I found surprising considering all that had gone on in Berlin over the preceding years.

I tentatively suggested that we should perhaps think about getting out of Berlin, but she gave me a resounding no. She had managed these last four years and she would manage the next. Nothing would make her leave, not even the Russians.

Soon it was Christmas which came and went without any celebration. There was absolutely nothing to celebrate or be joyful about.

Herta Schild – not sure of the year

As the forecasts had predicted, the weather in January was absolutely dreadful, freezing and so much snow. Life in Berlin was difficult enough, but this made it virtually impossible. Food was in short supply, even though many Berliners had left the city by this time, there were still horrendous food shortages and every single morsel was felt to possibly be the last. It was at this time that I personally witnessed an event during this horrific period that has stayed with me all my life. Rarely a day goes by when it does not pop into my mind again.

We knew things were bad and this incident, which occurred whilst I was staying with my mother, had a profound effect on me, at the time, and to this very day.

We were in the kitchen of Mutti's apartment when we could hear a commotion coming from the courtyard in the middle of the building. Of course, being nosey neighbours, we went out of the front door and peered over the balcony to find out what all the fuss was about.

In the yard, there were two SS officers who were talking extremely loudly with Frau Fischer, who had an apartment on the ground floor. With her was her son, Karl, who was about 12 or 13 years old. The SS officers were demanding to take Karl to join the Hitler Youth. Obviously, Frau Fischer was arguing that her son was far too young to be taken away and used for fighting. They grabbed the boy, who was in a dreadful state and in tears, trying as hard as he could to get back to his mother. The boy kept trying in vain to get out of the grasp of the SS officer, but he was being held too tightly.

Then, one of the officers took his sidearm out of the holster, aimed it at the boy's head and, without any hesitation whatsoever, pulled the trigger. Having shot and killed the boy, the officer, with no visible emotion, put his sidearm back in the holster. He then turned around, smiled at his colleague and the two of them simply walked off not saying a word or looking back at the utter desolation they had caused.

This act immediately brought home to me that we, as a nation, were utterly lost and obviously losing this entirely pointless war. We knew in our hearts that things were dreadful for Germany and we would, as a people, all be tarnished by the horrors inflicted on so many innocent souls.

The propaganda machine that had been driven at full force at the beginning of the campaign was now unnervingly silent. Like most Germans, at the outset of the war, I truly believed that Hitler was doing the best for our nation. But now we knew that it was all propaganda and we had been brainwashed with, in simple terms, a pack of lies.

There had been no bombing of Berlin for quite a few months but, on 3rd February 1945, the largest ever daylight bombing raid on Berlin was carried out by the USAAF. There were some 1,000 bombers and nearly 600 escort fighters of the Eighth Air Force. The end was close. I again desperately tried to persuade Mutti to leave Berlin with me. There was nothing left to stay for. But she steadfastly declined. No matter what I said, she refused to leave her home.

Having spent time with Erwin, I found him quite charming. He was full of stories and plans. He knew we must leave Berlin as there was nothing there for us any longer. He claimed that he had been offered a job in a small town to the west of Berlin and wanted me to go with him. He assured me that I would be safe and that once there he would be earning good money. Again, I begged my mother to go with us, but she continually refused – Berlin was her home, and no one was going to make her leave it, regardless of the risk.

We knew the Russians were approaching Berlin from the east at speed and it would not be long before they arrived. Reluctantly, and with a deep feeling of dread, I unwillingly left Mutti.

Erwin and I started the next phase of our journey to Lübbecke in Westphalia. Again, we knew the journey would not be easy as it was around 380 km to travel. I struggled so hard leaving Mutti in this dire situation, but she was adamant. I knew that there would be no persuading her so, unwillingly and with a heavy heart, I left her in Berlin and started on the journey westward with Erwin. Of course, it was bound to be difficult.

For this journey we had no travel documents. We had tried to get them before leaving Berlin, but it was impossible. The bureau where applications could be made was permanently closed due to bomb damage. Nevertheless, we thought it unlikely that we would be stopped by anyone in authority as basically many of the checkpoints were no longer in use.

We were heading straight towards the direction of the Allies who were pushing their way across France and Belgium into Germany on the way to their ultimate goal, Berlin. We must have been utter fools to even attempt this journey but knew that we must make the effort. We felt that to be caught by the Allies was a far better fate than being caught by the Russians. German forces were everywhere, hopelessly digging in to halt the progress of the Allies from the west and Russians from the east. But it would prove to all be in vain. Soon, this utterly pointless war would be at an end.

Many Berliners were fleeing the city as they knew that soon Germany would have no choice but to surrender. Erwin having a truck, with fuel, was incredibly fortunate. I asked him again where the truck and fuel containers had come from, but he simply brushed away my questions. I felt it better not to ask again. Erwin had made 'arrangements', which I assume probably included a monetary contribution, with three other Berliners and they joined us in the back of the truck for our perilous journey. We knew it could perhaps take a couple of weeks to make the journey. The roads were in a dreadful state: what with troop movements and bomb damage.

We finally started our journey just before my 25th birthday in February 1945. Rather than travelling on main routes we took cross-country rural routes. Erwin knew the area exceptionally well and we hoped by not travelling the expected route we could avoid the main troop movements.

Eventually, after five days we arrived in Lübbecke. It was a strange feeling after Berlin. Everything was relatively normal. No bombing damage, no German troops stationed in the town and people still going about their routine daily lives. Erwin found his contact/friend and, through him, arranged for basic accommodation for our little group. We settled down to a few weeks of relative calm.

The daily news was awful. Rumours were rife about atrocities that had been carried out by the Nazi regime. We still, in our hearts, had hoped that these heinous reports were scaremongering by the Allies. But deep down we were beginning to realise, to our shame, that the rumours were true.

Towards the end of March 1945, panic began to spread around the town. Scouts returned from their daily sorties and advised that the Allies were awfully close. It had been several days since we last saw any German troops passing through. We did not know what to do. On 1st April, armed with only a few provisions, the five of us went into the cellar of the house to hide. On the morning of the 3rd of April 1945, the Allies occupied the town. We were terrified. We did not know what to do. Should we stay hidden or reveal ourselves.

Three days after the Allies entered the town, Erwin crept upstairs to try to get an idea of what was going on. He came back quickly and told us that he managed to stay concealed but could see there were British troops outside in the street. No one in our group spoke English apart from me. After a brief discussion between us all, I was basically volunteered to go upstairs and into the street and surrender. We had no choice. Our small amount of provisions were gone. I was so very frightened.

Slowly, I made my way up the stone staircase from the cellar to the hall. I stood behind the front door for a few moments, catching my breath and deciding what to do. Finally, I thought the best would be to call out in English that I wished to surrender. So, I opened the door and shouted down the street. Immediately I was surrounded but not in the way I was expecting. I was greeted like a long-lost friend. The soldiers were so kind and helpful. They immediately asked if I was thirsty and I was given water.

Gradually, everyone came out of their hiding places and houses into the streets. The British troops found little resistance from the town folk. I think we all had simply had enough. Any firearms were collected but basically we were left in our homes but under arrest. It was a strange experience.

The events of the next few weeks seemed to occur in rapid succession, culminating on 30th April with the suicide of Hitler and Eva Braun. Hitler killed himself by gunshot in his Führerbunker in Berlin. Eva Braun, his wife of one day, committed suicide with him by taking cyanide. In accordance with Hitler's prior written and verbal instructions, that afternoon their remains were carried up the stairs through the bunker's emergency exit, doused in petrol and set alight in the Reich Chancellery garden outside the bunker.

On the 7th of May 1945, Germany surrendered unconditionally to the Allies. It was now all too apparent that Hitler was a psychopath who had orchestrated WW2 and The Holocaust that ultimately led to the deaths worldwide of some 40 million people.

Chapter 9

Not far from Lübbecke was the town of Bad Oeynhausen which became the headquarters of the British forces and British administrative authorities and military staff were housed in Lübbecke (BAOR – British Army of The Rhine). To that end, 251 of the 432 houses in the town were commandeered and cordoned off as accommodation for the Allies. Almost the entire town centre became an exterritorial zone and all the important administrative buildings of the town's infrastructure went to the British. The finance office on Herman Göring Straße (later Kaiser Straße) was used at the head office of the British Occupation Zone authorities.

Finally, the war was over but at a huge cost to Germany and the Allies. It all seemed so utterly pointless. It was now time to try and build our lives again but that was certainly easier said than done.

We occasionally had news from Berlin and knew my dearest Mutti was safe. It was estimated that 80% of Berlin historic buildings were lost. Reconstruction efforts in Berlin were incredibly slow. Much of the city was unsafe and uninhabitable, with large areas falling entirely into disuse. People were forced to make do, continuing their lives as best they could amid the destruction. Slowly, businesses got back underway but often in buildings that were missing walls and roofs.

As said before, Lübbecke was little affected by the war. The townsfolk quickly began to claw their way back to normality without much trouble.

One of the first things we all had to do was to be registered as a resident and be issued with Ausweis (identification pass). This was managed with the usual German efficiency at the town hall and all exceedingly bureaucratic and methodical though overseen by the British authorities. It was essential for the Allies to know who everyone was and, as we went about our daily business, often we would get stopped and asked to identify ourselves.

I never had a problem with this. The troops were always polite which, considering all that had happened in recent years, was somewhat surprising.

Of course, everything was still in short supply. The one person kept busy with this project was the town photographer, Herr Kühn of Foto Kühn. The Americans supplied the film and he had the job of photographing every single person in the town.

Personal details were recorded on a basic piece of paper with a photograph attached and stamped and signed by the records officer. This was a simple process and sufficed for the time being. I was issued with this rudimentary pass on the 16th of July 1945.

Ausweis 16th July 1945

Erwin and I had become close and I was eternally grateful to him for all he had done. I suppose, for all the wrong reasons, when he asked me to marry him, I said yes. I knew he probably was not to be trusted but we were living in a small town, which was largely Lutheran, and therefore it was completely unacceptable to not be married when living in the same property together.

On 17th November 1945, we married.

The job that Erwin was supposed to have did not materialise. He blamed the war and all the changes, but I concluded that there probably was not a job in the first place. He was a wheeler-dealer type, so it was not long before he found himself employed. He became a haulier. His truck came in handy and although fuel was nigh on impossible to get, Erwin, being Erwin, managed to get in with the transport section of the Allies.

We were now living in a small flat on Lange Straße in the centre of town. All we had were bare essentials and anything neighbours no longer wanted. We initially had no furniture. Neighbours donated a few bits and when Erwin went to Berlin for the Allies, I went with him. We were able to get a few pieces from his family.

When I had left Berlin in 1943 and moved to Hirschberg, Mutti had given me many of her 'good' things to take with me. But, having to leave there so abruptly in December 1945, these were all left behind. So, Mutti had very little left to give us but, what she could spare, we took with us.

The worst thing directly after the end of the war was rationing. We had only about 1100 calories each day. The British provided what they could, but most foods came from the Americans. We and the majority of Germans had no choice but to sell what we could so that we were able to buy essentials on the black market as it was impossible to live on the rations alone.

In early 1946, I decided to try and contact Dr Ullrich and see if was possible to obtain a reference from him. I needed to work, and it was always good to be able to show a new employer a good recommendation. Thankfully, he responded straight away.

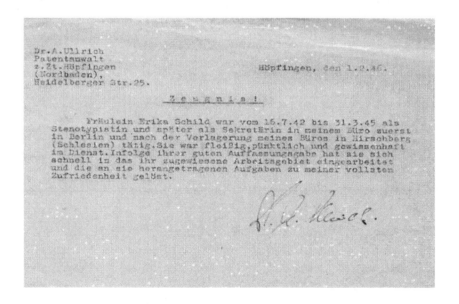

Reference Dr Arthur Ullrich

During this period of hardship, we did, however, occasionally get some respite. As already stated, earlier in my story, when I was at school, I excelled in English and began corresponding with a girl (Marietta Meyer) in the USA. From this simple beginning, we remained lifelong friends and an acquaintance that I cherish so incredibly dearly.

When we began corresponding in 1934, we would write to one another every couple of months. As teenagers, we had absolutely no interest in politics but would happily chat about school, family, movies and music. All too soon our friendship was put to the test with the outbreak of war. Corresponding during the war was not possible at all and I thought that maybe our friendship would not survive the horrors.

Once I was settled with Erwin, I decided that I should write to bring the Meyer family up to date with all that had happened to me and hope that maybe we could carry on where we left off. To my utter joy, a few weeks later, a letter came in reply. I was so apprehensive when I opened it. I prayed that all would be well and thank Heavens it was. Marietta and her family had not been affected in any great way by the war. Obviously, they knew families that had lost loved ones, but they themselves were all well.

Following this first letter, more arrived reasonably regularly along with parcels of things they thought we would need. They were well aware of the rationing and knew we were in desperate need so, as often as they could, they would send a package. Without a doubt, they were lifesavers and I am eternally grateful for their unstinting kindness.

The next incredibly special event in my life was the birth of my daughter.

It was on 28th June 1947, that my beautiful daughter was born and in recognition of the wonderful friendship I had with my pen friend in the USA, I named her Marietta. I am not sure why but, from the day she was born, she was always referred to as little Marietta. This stayed with her for a number of years before being dropped when she was around 9-10 years old.

Our lives continued as best as they could. It was not easy but as the months went by it did gradually become easier. The parcels from the USA continued to arrive and always with many wonderful things.

For instance, in May 1948, I received a letter and three parcels containing the following:

Peanut butter x 2

Dried beef x 2

Milk powder and egg powder

Lard and bacon

Peaches, jam and cocoa

Lavender soap x 3

Cookies and honey

Tablecloth x 1 and napkins x 6

Dishcloths x 3, tea towels x 3 and facecloths x 3

Stockings and shoes for me and Marietta a pullover

Wool and knitting needles

Little Marietta had a cold when these particular parcels arrived, and the honey was a Godsend. I used to put a little in her milk, and this definitely helped her improve. She loved anything sweet and, after she had eaten her supper, she was able to have a few cookies – such a very, very special treat.

The lavender soap was my treat and from the day the first bar arrived from the USA I continued to use Yardley lavender soap right up to this day. The scent from the soap was quite overwhelming and whenever we had visitors in our flat, they would invariably mention the lovely smell.

Bread and meat were two things still in short supply. But we had been promised that, following the harvest in 1948, more bread would be available. During 1948, the rationing began to ease up a little and we were now getting 500g of fat a month. The extra that the Meyer family sent us made such a massive difference.

Another major change in 1948 was to do with currency. The Reichsmark had been our currency since 1924 but now this was to be replaced. The Deutsche Mark was officially introduced on Sunday, June 20, 1948, by Ludwig Erhard, the Minister for Economic Affairs. The old Reichsmark and Rentenmark were exchanged for the new currency at a rate of DM 1 = RM 1 for the essential currency such as wages, payment of rents, etc., and DM 1 = RM 10 for the remainder in private non-bank credit balances, with half-frozen. Large amounts were exchanged for RM 10 to 65 Pfennig. In addition, each person received a per capita allowance of DM 60 in two parts, the first being DM 40 and the second DM 20.

A few weeks later, Ludwig Erhard, acting against orders, issued an edict abolishing many economic controls which had been originally implemented by the Nazis, and which the Allies had not removed. He did this, as he often confessed, on Sunday because the offices of the American, British and French occupation authorities were closed that day. He was sure that if he had done it when they were open, they would have countermanded the order.

The introduction of the new currency was intended to protect Germany from a second wave of hyperinflation and to stop the rampant barter and black-market trade (where American cigarettes acted as currency). Although the new currency was initially only distributed in the three western occupation zones outside Berlin, the move angered the Soviet authorities, who regarded it as a threat. The Soviets promptly cut off all road, rail and canal links between the three western zones and West Berlin, starting the Berlin Blockade. In response, the US and Britain launched an airlift of food and coal and distributed the new currency in West Berlin as well. This was a huge undertaking.

Only the air corridors on which the four victorious powers had agreed in the Air Agreement of 1945/46 were unaffected. For that reason, the three Western powers began an airlift to Berlin to supply the city and its approximately two million inhabitants with the necessities. It was an ambitious plan never before attempted on this scale and it was unclear whether it would work.

On June 28, 1948 the first American and British aircraft landed at Tempelhof and Gatow airfields with goods for the people of Berlin. Many other flights followed, but nobody could predict how long the blockade would last. For that reason, the Western powers initially planned to supply the city into the winter. The aim in the first weeks of the airlift was to fly 4,500 tons of goods into the city every day. This was raised to 5,000 tons a day in the autumn of 1948. Coal to meet the city's energy needs made up a large proportion of this tonnage.

In October, US General William H. Tunner was appointed to head the Combined Airlift Taskforce (CALTF), which had its headquarters in Wiesbaden. He perfected the airlift. The American military governor of Germany, General Lucius D. Clay, ensured the necessary political support of US President Harry S. Truman. Clay continually requested more and larger aircraft to use in the airlift, and Truman approved them.

In the first months of the airlift, the French occupying power participated with six airplanes. They urgently needed a third airport in Tegel in the French sector which was completed in November 1948. Some 19,000 workers built it in record time, taking just three months. The British mobilised their Royal Air Force and contracted with an additional 25 charter companies to fly mainly oil and gasoline into the city. Aside from their circa 23% share of the total airlift tonnage for freight, the British were also responsible for the lion's share of passenger transport during the blockade. With their C-54-transport planes, the US forces provided the largest air fleet for 'Operation Vittles', as the Americans called the mission. In spring 1949 the operation to supply Berlin was working so well that on some days more goods were flown into the city than had arrived before the blockade by road, water and rail.

The Western powers used the media effectively to publicise this outstanding efficiency. The continuing positive reporting on Allied tonnage and the growing reputation of the Western powers were certainly part of the reason for the lifting of the Soviet blockade on May 12, 1949. Despite the end of the blockade, the airlift continued for another four months into late summer 1949. The historical events known as the 'Berlin Blockade' and the 'Berlin Airlift' are thus chronologically not wholly identical.

The lifting of the blockade and the end of the airlift solved the first crisis of the Cold War by logistical means – without military force. This does not, however, mean that there were no casualties of the airlift. At least 78 people died in airplane accidents. Their names are engraved on the base of the Airlift Memorial in the Berlin district of Tempelhof.

The occupiers had become the protectors.

The Berlin Airlift palpably changed the relationship between the Western powers and West Berlin. Just a few years after World War II, the one-time enemies had mastered a severe political crisis by intensive cooperation. The population of Berlin now experienced the occupying powers as protecting powers.

Chapter 10

Yet another upheaval occurred on 23 May 1949, when The Federal Republic of Germany was founded in the west with the promulgation of the Basic Law. The first Bundestag elections are held on 14 August and Konrad Adenauer (CDU) became Federal Chancellor. The German Democratic Republic (GDR) was founded in the 'eastern zone' on 7 October 1949. Germany is in effect divided into east and west. However, Berlin had a special arrangement as a territory under Allied supervision (and kept that status until reunification on 3 October 1990). On 10 May 1949, the Parliamentary Council names Bonn the provisional capital of the new state.

These changes initially made visiting Mutti exceedingly difficult, but we were sure that as time went on it would become easier. Instead, we wrote to each other on a regular basis to keep in touch.

Mutti did not have a telephone or access to one but anyway, the GDR had blocked phones and cut off communication with the west so even if she had access to a telephone it would not have been any use. Therefore, letter writing was all we could do.

The next couple of years passed by quite quickly. Little Marietta was growing up and was such a sweet girl. Erwin was still working for the Allies in transportation. But all too soon, once again, my life was to be turned upside down.

I had always known that Erwin was a troubled soul. He lied relentlessly in order to get what he wanted. We often had rows as he would disappear for days at a time without letting me know where he was going or when he would be back. Then in July 1950, he disappeared for good. He walked out of his job, packed his clothes and a few other bits and pieces into his truck and left, never to return.

In my heart, I suppose I always knew this day would come. This was not going to defeat me. Over the past few years, I had dealt with far worse challenges. I knew the first thing I must do was to get a job. In the meantime, whilst looking for something, I used my skills of dressmaking and knitting to raise a few Marks. Trawling through junk shops and talking to neighbours I would collect any old jumpers, pullovers and cardigans. Each would be unravelled and the wool rolled into skeins. Then, I would knit them into something new and sell them. This kept the wolf from the door, but I was in desperate need of a proper job.

Since arriving in Lübbecke, I had become good friends with a couple called Frau and Herr Schmidt. They were born and bred in Lübbecke and exceptionally nice, kind people. Frau Schmidt offered to look after little Marietta whilst I was at work. She had two children of her own and said having another would not be a problem.

In September 1950, I started work as a typist and stenographer with Bund der vertribenen Deutschen (BVD). This was a non-profit organisation formed after the war to manage the estimated 13 to 16 million ethnic Germans who had been expelled from parts of Central and Eastern Europe. So many Germans had been displaced during WW2. Laws were being drawn up and passed granting citizenship to ethnic Germans. I carried on working for BVD until January 1953.

Marietta and Erika Schild in Lübbecke September 1953

In March 1953, finally, my divorce was granted due to desertion. It was good to have this settled but also it was incredibly sad. From the day Erwin left, he had never been in touch again. The one good thing to come out of my marriage was little Marietta. She was an absolute joy and a lovely child. She never caused me any problems. She was now at school and had made friends and was doing well with her learning.

One day, Frau Schmidt mentioned that she had heard that the British Army, still stationed in the town, was looking for locals who had a good command of English, both spoken and written. The money was good too, so I applied and thankfully, was taken on.

At the time, I was not to know that this one small act of accepting a new job would change my life forever.

Frau Schmidt would take care of little Marietta whilst I was working, so that was one great worry out of the way. Then came the real concern of working in a British Army facility. You must remember that the horrors of WW2 were still in our thoughts and the British were the recent enemy. Mind you, Lübbecke was inundated with British Army personnel out and about in the town and any that I had met had always been polite.

Although apprehensive, I was looking forward to this new beginning. The job was part-time from 9 am until 3 pm Monday to Friday. The location of the job was in Tax House and only about 10 minutes' walk from Lange Straße. However, I left home at 8:00 am to first walk to Wiehenweg, which was north of the town centre, to drop off little Marietta with Frau Schmidt, and then walk back into town. I did not want to be late and it was important for me to make a good impression on my first day.

As much as I knew about the job was that it was secretarial duties and liaison between British and German services. Not a great deal was explained to me at my interview, so I was not entirely sure what I would be expected to do but, whatever it was, I was determined to do the best I could.

Tax House used to be the Tax Office (Steueramt) for Lübbecke and stood on the then Hermann Göring Straße but now Kaiser Straße. Following the end of the war, it became the head office of the local British Zone Administration. The English translation from Steueramt became Tax House and everyone, including locals, knew it by its English name. The building was a large mansion in the centre of the town and some 3-4 kilometres from Tunis Barracks where most of the army personnel were stationed. The barracks was primarily home to an RCT

Sqn (later an Ambulance Tpt Sqn). The 2nd Armoured Division Signal Regiment (2 ADSR), who accompanied the Divisional Head Quarters on exercise and provided comms support, were located at Birdwood Barracks, Bünde.

I arrived at 8:50 am, suited and booted as best that I could. Thankfully, my sewing skills came in use again and I was incredibly lucky to have a number of suitable dresses to wear each day.

My hair had always been wavy and dark but now at the ripe old age of 33, it was already showing a few signs of grey. There was little I could do about it. Pointless trying to dye it as what was available was expensive and not particularly good. I was slim; well considering the years of rationing, there was no chance of putting on weight. I loved my high heels and had been saving a little in order to buy new shoes. For some reason, being in stockings, heeled shoes, a nice dress and a little lipstick, I felt good about myself.

I walked straight up to the main entrance where a soldier was on guard. He asked for my ID (ausweis) which I already had prepared in my hand. The old pass issued in 1945 had now been replaced with a more official-looking document.

Erika Schild Ausweis 24th September 1952 – aged 32

The guard asked why I was there, and I explained. He immediately took me inside.

There were several other local women working as secretaries. But, because my English was excellent, both verbal and written, I was to work on my own but for a number of English personnel. Though primarily for a Captain Meakes.

So far so good. Everyone was polite and helpful. English was the main language used in the building. It was a large building full of corridors and offices; the offices being numbered or named. There was also a canteen, kitchen, washrooms, meeting rooms and the officers' mess. The day-to-day routine was not exciting and much the same each and every day; managing the paper flow and liaison with outside sources.

However, a chance meeting on one of the corridors was to change my life, forever.

Chapter 11

Autumn had arrived. The leaves on the trees were falling and the green and warmth of the summer were gradually disappearing.

The year so far had been good. I was working, earning money and able to make ends meet. I was enjoying my job. Little Marietta was enjoying school and happy to go there every day. Sometimes her school friends would pop around to us in the afternoon after I got home from work to play together. All in all, things were not too bad now at all. Of course, little Marietta missed her dad. She was still far too young to understand what had happened. When Erwin first left, she thought it was because she had done something wrong. I reassured her that this was not the case at all. It was not easy for her but as time when on, it became easier.

Despite the awful history between our countries, the British were all kind to me and there was rarely a hint of animosity; well, not that I heard. One fateful morning, I was asked to urgently deliver some important papers to an office on the other side of Tax House to where my office was based.

Hurrying along a corridor, I rushed around a corner and bumped straight into a soldier coming the opposite way. He found it rather funny, but I was totally embarrassed. He immediately bent down, as I did, to help pick up the papers that had fallen. Quickly, I put the papers into some sort of order and apologising, said goodbye and carried on towards my destination.

I had absolutely no idea who the soldier was. But I did find him rather charming. He appeared quite a few years older than me, though I was then, and still am, absolutely no good at judging a person's age. He was what they used to call thick set – so not slim! Obviously, rationing had not been a problem for him. He had jet-black hair, vivid blue eyes behind tortoiseshell rimmed glasses and was extremely smart in his uniform with exceptionally shiny boots. He certainly had made an instant impression on me and I spent much of the day thinking about him and wondering who he was and if I would see him again.

Another day came to an end. I packed up my paperwork into the trays on my desk in preparation for the following day. I picked up my handbag, put on my coat and made my way out of the building hurrying to Frau Schmidt to collect little Marietta.

All the way there I was constantly thinking about the mysterious soldier. How ridiculous I was being. Why would he be interested in me – a German woman? I thought about his lovely kind blue eyes and when I might bump into him again.

But, despite keeping an eye out for him, two weeks went by and I did not see him at all. Then, one day, a knock on the door, it opened, and there he was standing in front of me.

He introduced himself. He was Staff Sergeant John Crowley of the RAPC based in room 63. He pronounced Crowley as in the bird, crow, and not as in the word 'our'.

Staff sergeant is the highest rank of a non-commissioned officer in the army.

I was like a teenager, utterly besotted from the outset. Heaven knows why. John was not by any means with movie star looks but he had a wonderful sense of humour and appeared to be a kind individual.

And so, it began. John had absolutely no reason whatsoever to come into my office but regardless of this, he would drop by. To be honest, I cannot remember much about this first conversation. I was all fingers and thumbs and blushing like you would not believe. As I have said, my English was perfect. But now that John was standing in front of me and talking to me, my command for the language all but disappeared. Thankfully, Captain Meakes appeared and John, making his excuses, vanished.

Over the next few weeks, John would often appear at random in my office. Usually just saying hello and disappearing again. Then one morning, he dropped by, said good morning and, to my astonishment, asked if I would like to have a drink one evening with him in the officers' mess. I truly was not sure about this at all and hesitatingly replied saying that I would think about it. That afternoon I went home feeling perplexed. What should I do?

I arrived at Frau Schmidt's to collect little Marietta and decided to ask Frau Schmidt what she thought I should do. Having explained the situation, she pondered for a while and then replied that I was single, and she could not think of any reason why I should not have a drink with this man – what harm could it do? I may have the drink with him and then decide that I did not like him after

70

all. I should go ahead as this would give me a much better understanding of John and I would then have a clearer idea of whether I wanted to see him again or just call it a day.

The next morning, as expected, John arrived at my office. By this time, I had got used to his footsteps along the corridor, so I knew he was on his way before he actually knocked on the door. As usual, he was smiling from ear to ear and exceptionally chirpy. Well, Erika, he asked, are you going to be brave and have a drink with me? I paused a few seconds before replying, yes John, that would be lovely.

We arranged to meet the following Friday evening at around 7 pm. Frau Schmidt had agreed to look after little Marietta, and I would collect her on Saturday morning. This was solely because I was expected that it would be quite late before I got back, and I did not want to disturb Frau Schmidt. Absolutely not for one moment did I imagine that I would be spending the night with John. That would not be right or proper in the least. I was, and remain, principled.

I had never been in the officers' mess, but I did know that one had to be well dressed. It was important for me to make a good impression. Choosing the right dress, shoes, makeup, perfume and hairstyle was crucial. Little Marietta was dropped off with Frau Schmidt on Friday morning, I worked my shift until 3 pm and then made my way straight home. This gave me a few hours to try and relax, have a bath and then get ready.

First, I decided what dress to wear and the accessories to go with it. I meticulously checked everything several times over to ensure that the whole lot was spotlessly clean and looking perfect. I laid out my clothes on my bed, then ran a bath. The lovely Meyers were still occasionally sending me parcels and as they knew my passion for lavender soap, they had also sent me some lavender oil for the bath. I dried myself off and, wrapped in a towel, dried my hair. Next a bit of makeup. Foundation first, then powder. My eyelashes were dark and long; therefore, I had no need to do anything with them. The final touch was a bright red lipstick.

My underwear was old but would of course do. It goes without saying that the dress I chose to wear, I had made myself. It was baby pink in colour with white polka dots. It had a V-neckline and a collar with a bow at the front. Tight-waisted with a swing skirt to just below the knee. Also, importantly, a voile net crinoline underskirt to give volume to my flared dress. Stockings and black brogue style shoes with block heels with a matching handbag completed the ensemble.

We had arranged to meet outside Tax House, and I made my way there with some trepidation. When I arrived, John was stood outside and, as I fully expected, he was looking incredibly smart. He greeted me with a warm smile, joking that he had thought that maybe I would change my mind and he was happy that I had been brave and came along. He complimented me on my dress and said that I looked incredibly beautiful.

Ever the gentleman, he took my arm and we entered the building. I walked into this building every working day but this time it seemed so different as we made our way to the officers' mess. John was constantly chatting. He was always so cheerful. We entered the mess and, of course, were immediately met by many prying eyes. A number of British servicemen had taken up with local girls. In the main it was accepted, but the heartache of war for many remained at the forefront of recent memories. Millions had died on both sides but the atrocities by some Germans were a stigma that was hard to bear.

John found us a corner table, asked me to sit down, and then enquired as to what I would like to drink. I decided on a small glass of white wine and John said he was going to have a pint of beer. John made his way to the bar to get our drinks and I sat waiting for him feeling incredibly nervous with the sensation that everyone was staring at me. Many of those there I saw each and every day. There were always polite to me. But now it seemed as though I was encroaching on their private British area and that I should not be there. I wanted to leave, run out and go back to my flat. Quickly, John returned with the drinks. Immediately, he saw the look on my face. He kindly reassured me and said that I should not be bothered at all. Time would heal. I then relaxed and we sat for a couple of hours chatting away about all sorts of everything.

Eventually, at around 11 pm, I decided that I should make my way home. John immediately offered to walk me back to Lange Straße. When we arrived, he shook my hand, said he had a lovely evening and hoped we could do the same again quite soon. I turned around, let myself in the front door, glanced at him to say goodbye and quickly shut the door. I think I then fell against the inside of the door feeling utterly relieved that the evening had gone so well.

Over the coming weeks, we met on a regular basis. We often would go for walks taking little Marietta with us. The countryside around the town was beautiful. The two of them got on so very well which was a blessing. My German friends accepted the friendship, but we occasionally came against animosity from some British personnel. We overcame that as we became closer. I was falling in love with this man and he with me.

Chapter 12

The letters. As our relationship developed, I began to receive letters from John. They were generally on paper which had on the top 'Writing Paper For The Allied Forces' and at the bottom saying that the stationery had been supplied by 'Society Of Assortments Factories Le Locle Switzerland'.

Often, they were typed, and John was reasonably proficient in this skill. Sometimes they would be left on my desk for me to find though usually, he would get a 'runner' to bring them to my flat on Lange Straße. A runner is basically a person who was asked to deliver/pick up paperwork or goods. Obviously, John should not have used this service for personal reasons but, being naughty, he did.

Invariably, John would start them and finish them in different manners. At times, he titled himself as 'The Very Reverend John Crowley, Command Pay Office, BAOR 42'. There were many letters though sadly a number have disappeared as the years have passed by. I now have in my box around 60 between us both.

The oldest letter is dated Wednesday 10th March 1954. The envelope is printed with On His Majesty's Service and John has handwritten Frau Erika Gerath, Prima Donna, Lübbecke. Inside there are two sheets of paper. Both are typed. One only goes down half the sheet and the bottom has been torn off though it is clear that there was nothing further typed because the tear is at an angle. This is not dated, and I cannot remember whether it came with the letter it is enclosed with or if it was sent at another time. But the content is truly incredible, and I especially want to share all with you. So, following is this letter together with a few of the other ones that I received during this first year of our courtship.

They contain the most beautiful sentiments. I've no idea why the first one is simply a fragment. It may be that he got to where he did and simply never finished it. But generally, once every month a letter arrived and each with similar sentiments. I was utterly smitten with this truly remarkable man. He was so kind and understanding. All he wanted to do was cherish and look after me and little Marietta.

I never knew when to expect the next letter. Invariably, they were filled with day-to-day banter but, importantly, incredibly descriptive of his love for me. I was utterly captivated by his attention and quickly it was all too apparent that I too was developing strong feelings towards him. How could I not? His words in the letters were quite wonderful, and that is an understatement, as I find it incredibly hard to convey how extraordinarily special they were. And when I was with him, he spoke the same directly to me.

I was sure I was falling in love with this man. However, one thing often contained in the letters which I was never that impressed with was a doodle of a cat from the rear – with a dot for its bottom! I do not know why this never pleased me, but I did not like it. But, regardless of my feelings towards these cats, they continued to often be included.

Read them and you will instantly see why falling in love with this man was so easy. He could not have said more delightful and astonishing words to me. I cherished his words from the first letter until this day.

WRITING PAPER FOR THE ALLIED FORCES

My Dearest,Darling,Iriss,

If this wretched typewriter holds with me I shall be able to tell you how much I love and cherish you,that I love you until it hurts me so much,and yet you still do not believe me,when I say that it is you that I want or ever shall want for that matter,but then of course I do understand that certain circumstances do prevail,circumstances that I certainly hope we shall be able to surmount at an early date so my darling I do hope that you will bear with me and above all have faith in me my darling.

Though I have known you but a short time,I feel that really I have known you all my life,that always you have been waiting round the corner,just waiting,as though we were bound to meet,and now that we have,let us please reap the full benefits of such a warm and generous love,a love that mortals such as us can only have at one life time,do not let us of course be too hasty,but above all do not let us leave things too late,let us sample full love as only two who I am sure love each other so dearly should so rightly have.

It is well known that many affairs of the heart come to people during their lives,and so often it is just a passing fancy that draws two beings together,I pray that in our case it is not just that passing fancy,but something that we can cherish for the rest of our days,something that we can look back on in the future,as something that has been accomplished,for which there are no regrets,love can be very strange at times,but whatever nationality one is,no matter what race,indeed,if the love is true and lasting,nothing can come wrong,only true

Command Pay Office,
BAOR 42.

27th.April,1954.

Mina Liebling,Mine Frau,Mine Apple Blossom,and mine everything that is sweet and
beautiful l ike my Erica,

How is my preious little Pet this morning,this very bright and Sunny morn,do
you get up nice and early,despite the fact that you are on holiday,you know Erica I do
envy you a trifle,being on holiday and the weather so grand,and here is poor me still
at the grindstone,hard at it as usual?????????????.

I imagine that this little note will come as a surprise to you,it also surprises
me to realise that I am writing to you,especially during working hours,the answer of
course is that I am having an easy time,and also that I did miss your sweet face this
morning at the office and also on my going to dinner,however my Pet I shall be seeing
you in the evening and also when we go to the pictures.

At the moment I have just got my morning cup of tea in,and also two Berliners,do
you understand that,I must keep up my health and strength,otherwise our love will
suffer and that would not do at all would it??.I expect you will be having your usual
cup of coffee,lucky girl,try and save me a cup for say Wednesday afternoon,for I have
decided with your permission that we have a ramble on that afternoon,weather permitting
of course,I think this time we shall be able to get to the top of the hill,not like
on Sunday when you gave up so easily???????????.

Now my brown eyed witch,what now,I must impress on you that you should not waste
too much of your time doing washing for that lazy old reprobate,just a quick dash in
the water,out and press all in five minutes,that will leave you plenty of time to have
a spot of something for you lunch then out,in the fresh air,it works wonders ,And I am
sure you need it,the fresh air I mean,always sitting in a wretched office,or in the
mess till late at night,then to rush home and get into bed,incidently almost alone,I
was going to say alone,but I remembered Marietta just ine time,so you see my lovely you
waste most of your life by sitting,working,sleeping and rushing home ???,you will have
to alster this mode of life and indulge in the beauty of fresh air,does this seem so
much nonsense to you,I am not certain what I think about it,one thing is certain,that
is that I love you an awful lot,cant do without you now,though where it is all going to
end I cannot see,but we must not let our love diminish,we must at all times and for
ever be the same tow ards each other,otherwise my life will be empty and without hope,
so my darling do try and be the same as you are now for allways.

Well my Lotus Blossom In must call a halt,at last I have work to do,not much but
something to keep me quiet for the time being,so I will say cheerio,

Lots of love,

yours, John

XXXXXXXXXXXXXXXX

Command Pay Office,
Sunday, 16th.May,1954.

My Darling of Darlings,

What better day could I pick to write to my darling one,and what a glorious day it/ is,how I wish that I wre able to be out with you,and so enjoy all that is to be offered by this glorious sunshine,never mind my pet there will be other days,and not so far distant, though alas we shall not be able to enjoy a Sunday afternoon walk for at least two more weeks,what a pity it is that I am in so much demand these days,that is the penalty of being so clever ?????????????????.

I wonder what you are doing at this very moment,busy with the cooking I should imajine,though I think that on Sunday you do not eat so very much,if I wre you I would take things very easy,especially in view of the fact that you had a very busy evening,last e vening ???????????,by the way have you lost your cold,you should have after such grand excitement.

At this moment,well not exactly this moment,but a little before this I had been having a grand fight with the transport people,theres always trouble over transport,more so on Sunday(s,everything seems to go wrong when I am on duty,but should I worry,so long as everything goes all right with us,that is the main point,that we should enjoy life to the full,and do you know I really think that it will turn out that way,at the moment things are mixed up,I expect you are wondering whno things will come to a head,though you usver mention how things are going,so far as my maternal affairs are concerened,actually I cannot tell you much,at the moment things are almost at a standstill,which cannot be helped,the law always takes a devil of a time to get cracking,but my darling all is bound to come out all right for two that are so much in love with each other as you and I are.

Darling I have never loved anyone the same as I do you.I know that my life has been full of women,what mans has not,but with you it is something so ver differant,what it is I cannot explain,all I know is that I must be near you at all times,and when I am I alway lose my head as it were,I never really know whether I am on head or my heels,what is the spell that you have cast over me,there is certainly something about you that gets me going, it must be your lovely brown eyes,now dont you dare say they are not brown,or am I clour blind as well as sh ort sighted,no I am long sighted I think,but what ever colour they are the they are wonderfull the same as you my darling,how I am hoping that I cann live up to what you want me to be,though the pedestal that you want reaching is very high,I wonder really if I have the stuff in me that makes such a great man as you want,anyhow one can but try,that is all that I can do.

Dinner time has arrived,wha t are you going to serve me,one of those delicious steaks that I once had at your place,whata hope,I shall have to be contented today with a little of what the mess has to offer,and just imajine that you have cooked the dinner and that it is wonderfull,it will bound to taste delightfull then,my darling of darlings.

What a lost of nonsense I seem to be writing,though I can assure you My dearest Eri ca that it is not my intention to write silly,but then true love always at all times does seem so silly when put on paper,but I can assure you sweetheart of mine that I mean veryword that I have typed,do try ahd believe me,for once in ny life I am trying to be so honest and loveable to one who I love so very dearly,and on that score I must conclude,I am patiently waiting for you to arrive this afternnon and evening,then once again I shall have you so very near to me,so cheerio my sweet one,

all my love to you,

ever yours, John

xxxxxxxxxxxxxxxxxxxx
xxxxxxxxxxxxxxxxxx
xxxxxxxxxxxxx

PS Please do not chide me over the rotten typing,afterall I am only a learner.

COMMAND PAY OFFICE,
BAOR. 42.

CPO/LOVE/DELIRIOUS.

28th.June,1954.

Erica,My Love,

　　　　　I wonder why I am always writing letters to you when I am on duty,of course the same as you I have very little spare time to think of letter writing,apart from when I am on duty,even now I have not the slightest idea of what I am going to say to you,I do wish that I could think of something that would be differant,but all I can think of is love and lo love and more love,it is strange how one can be attracted to one of the oppostie sex and be willing to defy the world for her,theres something about you that I just cannot fathom, I have known so many women in my life,that is natural I suppose,or is it,perhaps it is too bad to have too many romances,but one thing I do know is the fact that never before have I been so much in love as I am with you,is it that you are a witch,so that you can cast spells over me,you certainly do something that rather unerves me,shall I ever get out of your spell I certainly hope not,though were I to leave tomorrow,I would cherish the thought that I have at last,or rather at least lived for the past eight or so months,and my sweetheart do believe me,I am really terribly greatfull that I have had the privilege of having you for a companion,yes even more than a companion,an understanding loveable woman,I pray that we shall always be able to continue for the rest of our lives.

　　　　　What I would like to do is to get you away to England,even now but of course that cannot be so,we shall have to wait a bit,but I do hope that before long things will be much clearer and I shall be able to take you and provide a home for you,of course I understand dearest,that I am asking a lot of you,I sometimes wonder what on earth you see in me,why should you bother so much over me,afterall I have at the moment nothing at all to offer you,I have no home,no family,why I am just an orphan,of course we are still quite young,I infact at times feel younger than you,that is only by reason of my love,my deep, deep love for you,what a great thing it would have b.en,had we met many years ago,what a plended life we would surely have had,however now we shall have to make the best of things as only you and I at you side can do.

　　　　　Now my lovely,I think that I have said quite enough for this time,afterall you will be seeing me this evening,and see that you behave yourself,or should it be on the other foot,I should behave myself,but then do I ever misbehave myself,only when I get too tired,and I do get tired,but of course not too tired,one thing I must ask you darling is that when I do get tiresome,please try and help me,I cannot help it really,I do try my best to be pleasing at all times,especially where you are concerned,and I always seem to blot my copy-book at times,thank heavens you are so understanding.

　　　　So cheerio my honey-bunch,will be seeing you,

　　　　　　all my fondest love,ever yours,

　　　　　　　　　　　John
　　　　　　　　　　　　　xxxxxxxx
　　　　　xxxxxxxxxxxxxxxxxxxxxxxxxxxxxxxxx

Statinnery offered by:

FRAMONT WATCHES

78

Wednesday,21st.July, 1954.
Somewhere in Germany.

Erica my Darling,

Once again duty calls,so naturally you are due for another of my duty letters,though what I am going to write about I have not the slightest idea,I reckon though by the time that I have got underway I shall have put something on paper that will be of interest to you,firstly I must comment on this ruddy typewriter,its all yours and why it it should stick as it does is beyond me,I suppose the reason is that with all the work that you do with it and the speed tht you set up that is really the cause of all the trouble, apart from the fact that I am the worlds worst typist.

However Darling let me get forward with my letter,I wonder what it is that you attract me so much with,why am I always,trying to be near you and wanting you so much, why do I love you so much that it almost hurts,why is it my darling of darlings,why is that the mere touch of you sends me all haywire,why do you do all these certain lovely things for me,and when you love me,why do I feel as I have never felt before,can it be true and real love that we have for each other,surely it cannot be anything else but a great love, a love that I am praying can never,never cease.

When I look back over the years,I wonder why it was not me lot to meet such a grand companion as you are,and what makes it all the more strange is the fact that it did really take a War to bring us together,but then I am a believer in Fate,and I am certain that at some time in our lives we would have bound to have met ,no matter what the circumstances,and now dear one,now that I have found you I do want to keep you,I wish that I could offer you more than I do,but my life is perhaps nearer the end than the beginning, if you can follow what I mean,afterall I am not so very young,though on the other hand I am not so old,what I am really trying to say,that it will be very difficult to start again as if I were say thirty,places do not come easy,in that I meant finding a good home for you,one thing I am sure of is that if we pull together we are bound to come out on top, no matter where we finish up.So all I ask my sweet is to try and trust in me,please darling do try very hard,I know I am perhaps asking a lot,more than I dare to think of.

Another three and a quarter hours before I can be near you,it seems an age,I am already counting the minutes,and are they going slowly,always am I suffering,but I suppose I must not grumble,you will probably be suffering also before you got home, bless you darling,for allowing me to get you to the state when you do suffer on my account, happy suffering sweetheart.

Before I conclude this letter,I must mention darling the times when I am most tiresome to you,but dear one here I must blame the weather,youb have no idea how ill I feel when the weather is heavy and there is plenty of cloud and rain,I feel absolutely awfull,so darling when I am like that and am being short tempered with you,try and remember that I am not trying to hurt you in any way,its just that I cannot even bear myself.

So now another short note to my loved one is ending,cheerio my
precious one precious one,all my love to you,

John N.C.

xxxxxxxxxxxxxxxxx XXXX

Germany,
17th. October, 54.

Darling, Darling, *Elsie*

Though I have started this letter, I have not the foggiest idea of what I am going to write about, how does one commence to write to ones loved one, infact I could hardly put to paper how much I love you, I could not express myself firmly enough, there are no words to express my full love and endearment for you.

One thing I can say, is to quote a very old qotation, "Never has a Wowan given a man so much happiness over a year"as you have, I cannot understand what it is draws you to me or I to you, surely it cannot be anything but true love, when I mention these things I do so with a strange feeling inside me, wondering whether things will

continue to remain the same as the years go by, and I earnestly pry that they do, I could not possibly go oh at all without you, and I yhink I am right in saying that you think on the same lines, it must be so otherwise we could not act as we do now. This love of ours is not something that is here on a temporary basis, it is something that can only be permanent and lasting, so darling of mine, let us hope and hope and pray

hard that for ever we shall be as ohe, and defy the world and its troubles with all our might and fortitude.

I wonder what you are doing at this very moment, my thoughts go back to last week, how I would have loved that to have been yesterday, or rather yesterday evening, it would not have mattered if I had to leave to go on Duty, I would have had the pleasure of your undying love, and the warmth of your sweet body to console me in memories whilst working hard at this wretched Tax House.

This my lovely is all that you are going to get this time, I am just away to my lunch, but I am waiting patiently for the nine o'clock hour to arrive, when I can see your sweet face again.

So Cheerio my lovely, hurry up and get here,

SOCIETY OF ASSORTMENTS
FACTORIES
LE LOCLE (Switzerland)

I am ever yours,

your devoted lover,

80

John also sent me these few lines of poem in his October letter – he was not particularly good at rhyming.

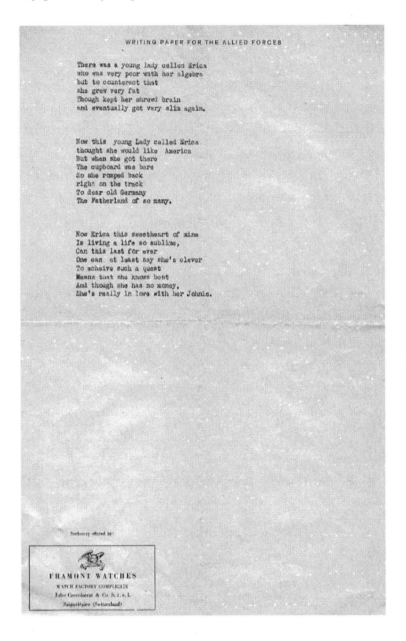

On 27th March 1954, John had been awarded the Meritorious Service Medal and Annuity. In the autumn of the same year, an incredibly special event occurred, and I was able to share this wonderful occasion with him.

The event was recorded in the RAPC journal at the time as follows:

At the Command Pay Office, BAOR 42 (Lübbecke), the occasion of the birthday of Her Majesty The Queen was celebrated by a parade of troops of the Lübbecke Garrison. The RAPC contingent, under the command of Major D.O. Hood, was deemed the smartest on parade. The highlight of the parade was the presentation by the District Commander of the Meritorious Service Medal to Staff Sergeant John Crowley, to whom we extend hearty congratulations.

To be awarded the MSM, an individual must have 'good, faithful, valuable and meritorious service, with conduct judged to be irreproachable throughout'. They must have at least twenty years' service and already hold the Long Service and Good Conduct Medal. The number of MSMs awarded is limited: no more than eighty-nine in the army a year and in practice this number is not reached. I was so incredibly moved by the whole event and especially excited for John. It was a great honour to receive such recognition.

Parade in Lübbecke autumn 1954 – John is on the far right in front of the car

John Crowley MSM presentation, autumn 1954

John was awarded five medals during his army career and proudly wore them on special occasions whilst serving and after he retired.

They are as follows:

Efficiency Medal	Awarded 11th October 1946
Defence Medal	Awarded 11th October 1946
War Medal	Awarded 11th October 1946
Long Service & Good Conduct	Awarded 18th May 1953
Meritorious Service Medal	Awarded 27th March 1954

Chapter 13

Our life in Lübbecke was reasonably good during the mid-1950s. Rationing was a distant memory and all the things that were in short supply were now available in abundance.

Berlin was often in my thoughts as Mutti was still there and in the same apartment on Schöneweider Straße. She was getting on in age and her health was not good.

By 1954, visiting had become extremely difficult. The GDR made travel and communications between West and East Germany incredibly challenging. I could still get to Berlin by train, but it was a convoluted, long and tiring journey. First, I had to take a little local train from Lübbecke to Bünde. Then a mainline train to Hannover. There I would change again onto a train to Berlin. Leaving the West for the East meant numerous border checks. All extremely bureaucratic, long-winded and painful but in order to see Mutti, it had to be endured.

Little Marietta came with me on one occasion and thoroughly enjoyed the trip. I suppose it was an adventure for her. Whilst in Berlin, I took the opportunity to visit Erwin's parents and introduce them to little Marietta. We had exchanged the occasional letter and they had made it clear they would love to meet their granddaughter. We never ever heard from Erwin from the moment he deserted us and neither had his parents.

We were long-time divorced and one thing that did upset me was that he had no contact at all with little Marietta. She was but a baby when he abandoned us and whatever the issues between us, the adults, he was quite wrong to cut little Marietta out of his life. But now she had John as a father figure and the two of them were great mates.

Overall, John and I seemed to have a perfect relationship though I did perhaps have a couple of concerns. One being that he was quite a few years older. But the major problem that I had great difficulties with and found incredibly hard to rationalise was the fact that John was married and had two grown-up boys. I trusted John implicitly but had only known him a relatively short time.

In 1954, John was 49 years old and I was 34. Therefore, it was probably not unexpected that he should be/had been married. John explained that he had not lived with his wife in many years. They had two sons, Gary and Michael. He adored his boys but the relationship with their mother was not an easy one.

John met and married Alice in Canterbury, Kent, England. At the time, John was serving in the Buffs (Royal East Kent Regiment), which were based in the city. John and Alice married in on the 26th of December 1933. Garrington Thomas David (always known as Gary) was born on 1 March 1936, and Michael Ronald John followed on 17th September 1939.

Gary and Michael Crowley – John's boys

John spent a lot of time away serving in the army and I suppose Alice was lonely. One of John's army pals, Ernie, had recently separated from his wife, had left the army and had nowhere to live. John suggested he get in touch with Alice as they had a spare room at their house on Athelstan Road in Canterbury and he could lodge there. Of course, the inevitable happened and Alice and Ernie had an affair. Obviously, John was upset but quickly resigned himself to the fact that he was no longer wanted. Ernie took over hook, line and sinker. John though steadfastly refused to give Alice a divorce. Alice and Ernie lived as husband and wife, but legally, they were not.

Also recorded in John's army records is another son, Paul Nicholas Robert, born on 27th November 1947. Although he is detailed as being John's son, he was not. He was the son of Alice and Ernie.

Once my relationship with John began to gain momentum and develop, we discussed his getting divorced. I could not continue with our relationship knowing he was married and not working towards a divorce. Finally, John agreed. He got in touch with Alice and arrangements began. It was not an easy task. Alice had committed adultery and John had persistently refused to divorce her because of this. But he was now in love with me and wanted us to marry so he started to move the proceedings along. We knew that it would take quite a while before a court hearing but at least things were moving forward.

John never spoke at all about his own family; well, not his mother and father. Once, I did ask but was abruptly stopped from asking further questions. It was obvious that he had no wish whatsoever to discuss them. As far as I knew his parents were no longer alive and he was an only child.

He told me that he grew up in Folkestone which is a small port town on the English Channel in Kent, in the South East of England. The town lies on the southern edge of an area in England known as the North Downs at a valley between two cliffs. It was an important harbour during the 19th and 20th centuries and one of the closest points to France, the coastline of which can be seen on a clear day.

He lived with his grandmother Eliza, his uncle Charles and his mother, Emily, at 21 Darby Road in Folkestone. He attended Christs' Church School, Folkestone, which was only a short walk away and appeared to have had a reasonable education. It was here that his love of football developed – something that remained with him all his life. But his one childhood wish was to join the army as soon as he could. Whether this wish emerged from incidents or effects from WW1 he never disclosed.

Christ Church School football team. John is back row, fourth from right

As soon as he was able, he made the journey from Folkestone to Canterbury, also in Kent, to join up. The distance between the two places was around 50 km and the easiest way to get there was by train.

Canterbury is a beautiful city and an important one in English history. It is a historic cathedral city and a UNESCO world heritage site. The cathedral, which is situated in the centre of the city, was founded in the year 597 and completely rebuilt between 1070 and 1077. It is truly the most remarkable building and steeped in history.

As soon as John arrived in Canterbury, he made his way to the enrolment offices. What I did not know at the time when he was telling me all this information was that, when he made the journey, he was only 16 years old. He was born on the 19th of April 1907, but according to his army records, his date of birth was recorded as 19th April 1905! This fact remained a complete secret for the rest of his life. Even I was totally unaware of this 'error'. He told me the same as was on his army records that he was born in 1905, and so when we met, I believed he was 49 years old when in fact, he was only 47.

He enlisted for seven years on 24th April 1923 (which he extended pretty quickly), only a few days after his 16th birthday, and was allocated his service number of 6282090.

From reviewing John's army records many years later and researching if he did have any relatives, there are a few things that always make me smile. On enlisting he was shown as being 5ft 7in tall. But, two years later, this had changed to 5ft 9 ¾ in. Obviously, being so young, he was still growing. His trade prior to enlisting was detailed as a hairdresser.

According to John's birth certificate, he was born John Nicholson Crowley. His mother's name was noted but there was nothing for the father. During my research, I discovered that the details of next of kin shown on his army records of Mrs E Crowley, an aunt, of Wythenshawe, Saltwood, Kent were not accurate. This was actually John's mother who was in domestic service with a family in Saltwood whose surname happened to be Nicholson.

I can only assume that he was probably the result of a dalliance between his mother and someone in the household. This was not an uncommon occurrence in those days. Domestic staff were often put upon by their employers and little could be done. However, I think that possibly the 'father' did take some responsibility as John had a good schooling.

As I said earlier, he never ever spoke of his mother or father and acted as though they were both long dead. But this was not the case. He was illegitimate and that would have been a significant embarrassment and extremely shameful at the time. I suppose it was easier to consider her dead than to explain his family history.

Emily Margaret Crowley taken in 1918 – aged 32

Chapter 14

And so, his long career in the army had begun. He commenced his training and further education in Canterbury but soon transferred to London.

Although, as I said, his education was reasonable, he had further education care of the army. He attained a third-class certificate on 25th May 1923, and then a first-class certificate on 15th May 1924.

His first posting abroad was to Egypt on 5th December 1924 but only for a short time. He then moved along the Mediterranean to Gibraltar from 24th March 1925 until 6th February 1927. From Gibraltar, he moved on to India and remained there until 7th November 1930.

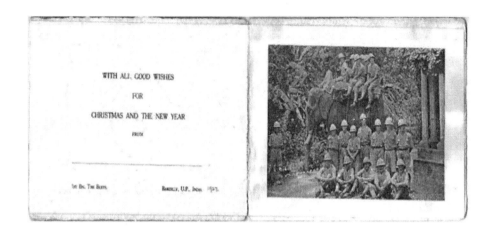

The Buffs Christmas card 1927

Then it was back to the UK until 23rd April 1935, when he came to the end of his enlistment time. John had no intention of leaving the army. Having been discharged, he immediately began to plan to re-enlist. He made his way back to Canterbury to Alice. Then virtually straight away, he returned to the recruiting office and on 21st May 1935 re-enlisted but this time in the RAPC – Royal Army Pay Corps. I do not know whether he had had enough of active service and wanted a desk job, but this is what he re-enlisted for.

And then on to more training. On 21st May 1936, he was promoted to corporal and then to lance corporal on 29th November 1937, and promotion again on 21st May 1938, to staff sergeant.

Then on to the fateful date of 1st of September 1939, and the onset of WW2. John was posted in December 1939 to Hastings in Kent and there he remained for the majority of WW2. He was promoted again to acting sergeant major for the duration of the war.

Hastings is a seaside town and borough in East Sussex on the south coast of England, 39 km east to the county town of Lewes and 85 km southeast of London. The town gives its name to the Battle of Hastings, which took place 13 km to the north-west at Senlac Hill in 1066. It later became one of the medieval Cinque Ports (Hastings, New Romney, Hythe, Dover and Sandwich). In the 19th century, Hastings was a popular seaside resort, as the railway allowed tourists and visitors to reach the town.

On 12th August 1943, he was again posted to India and he remained there until May 1945.

This period of time in India was known as The British Raj. This system of governance was instituted on 28 June 1858, when, after the Indian Rebellion of 1857, the rule of the British East India Company was transferred to the Crown in the person of Queen Victoria (who, in 1876, was proclaimed Empress of India). It lasted until 1947 when it was partitioned into two sovereign dominion states: The Dominion of India (later the Republic of India) and the Dominion of Pakistan (later the Islamic Republic of Pakistan, the eastern part of which, still later, became the People's Republic of Bangladesh).

At the inception of the Raj in 1858, Lower Burma was already a part of British India; Upper Burma was added in 1886, and the resulting union, Burma (Myanmar), was administered as an autonomous province until 1937, when it became a separate British colony, gaining its own independence in 1948.

Whilst in India on this occasion, he was based in Allahabad which is in the north of the country in the state of Uttar Pradesh. I still have a number of souvenirs that he brought back. He must have visited the theatre on a couple of occasions and kept the programs. He also kept a scrappy Christmas menu that is signed by all those in attendance. It is, unfortunately, now in extremely poor condition as seen here.

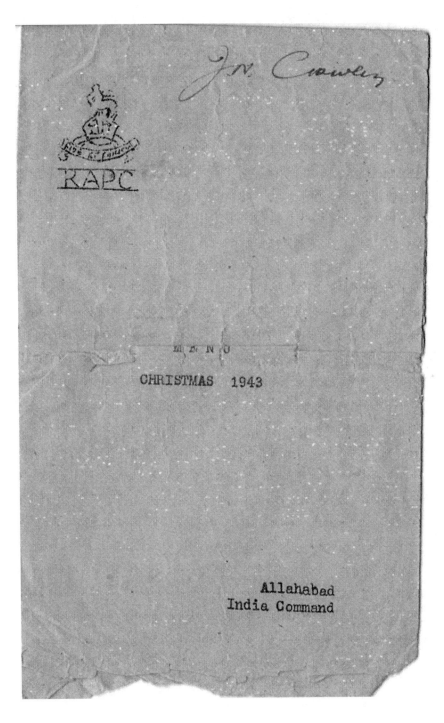

RAPC Allahabad Christmas menu 1943

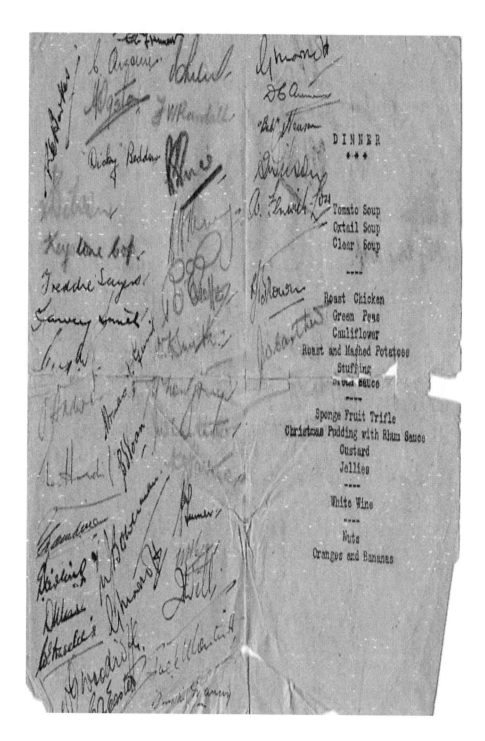

DINNER
***

Tomato Soup
Oxtail Soup
Clear Soup

Roast Chicken
Green Peas
Cauliflower
Roast and Mashed Potatoes
Stuffing
Bread Sauce

Sponge Fruit Trifle
Christmas Pudding with Rhum Sauce
Custard
Jellies

White Wine

Nuts
Oranges and Bananas

RAPC Allahabad Christmas menu 1943

94

FRENCH

without

TEARS

A Comedy by TERENCE RATTIGAN

GARRISON THEATRE

McPHERSON BARRACKS

ALLAHABAD

THURSDAY 8-45 p. m.

14th December, 1944

Seat G 9

I know little of what John experienced during WW2 as he never discussed in any detail. Whether because I was German, or whether because he experienced/witnessed awful things, I do not know. I am certain that millions in England as well as Germany were affected by something during this utterly atrocious period in world history and did not want to share their memories. John returned back to the UK In May 1945 and immediately went back to Hastings.

RAPC Hastings May 1946

John's time in the army came to an end again and he was discharged on the 2nd October 1946. He kept this tatty discharge certificate. No idea why this was not issued until 6th February 1947, or why the cause of discharge says services no longer required on re-enlistment because he re-enlisted the next day on 3rd October 1946.

DISCHARGE CERTIFICATE.

Army Form B103J

(If this CERTIFICATE is lost no duplicate can be obtained.)

Army Number...... 6282090

SURNAME...... CROWLEY

CHRISTIAN NAMES ...... JOHN NICHOLSON

Effective Date of Discharge...... 2 OCTOBER 1946

Corps from which Discharged ......

...... ROYAL ARMY PAY CORPS

Service with the Colours : Years...... 7 ......Days...... 49

Service on Class W(T) Reserve : Years...... 4 ......Days...... 86 [SUPPLEMENTARY]

Total Service : Years...... 11 ......Days...... 135

Rank on Discharge ...... STAFF SERJEANT

Cause of Discharge ...... SERVICES NO LONGER REQUIRED ON RE-ENLISTMENT

Campaigns and Service Abroad...... INDIA., 12 AUGUST 1943 TO 4 MAY 1945

Medals ...... EFFICIENCY MEDAL (MILITIA) ...... DEFENCE MEDAL

Military Conduct ...... Exemplary

2381

Signature and Rank
Officer i/c Records.

Date...... 6 FEBRUARY 1947 Place...... THE WAR OFFICE, F.9(a)

(5,0308) Wt. 51092/4985 42,000 2/45 Hw, G.51-9999

Around this time, John must have visited an unemployment office (nowadays a job centre) just in case he had reason to sign on the dole. I am only mentioning this because he must have been given the following document which is a notice to claimants. I have included as I thought the content might be of interest. Earnings must not exceed 6/8d (six shillings and eight pence) on the day in question, which in today's money is around 48p so not much at all. This form was in circulation between 1934 and 1948.

NATIONAL INSURANCE ACTS

UNEMPLOYMENT BENEFIT

NOTICE TO CLAIMANTS

READ THIS LEAFLET CAREFULLY AND KEEP IT FOR REFERENCE. Each time you draw benefit you will sign a declaration that you have read it and understand its contents. If in doubt on any point, ask at the Employment Exchange. For further information ask for Leaflet N.I. 12. Be sure to inform the Employment Exchange at once if you CHANGE your ADDRESS.

BENEFIT FOR YOURSELF

1. **Declaration upon claiming.** When you sign the Unemployed Register Form on pay day you are declaring that on the days for which you have signed

(1) you were unemployed ; and

(2) you were capable of and available for work ; and

(3) you satisfied the other benefit conditions set out in this leaflet, including the Overlapping Benefits provisions described in paragraph 2.

2. **Overlapping Benefits.** You must tell the Employment Exchange if you are getting, or have claimed, or anybody else is getting, or has claimed on your behalf, any payments under the National Insurance or Industrial Injuries schemes, or a Government Training scheme, or if you have a disability pension or allowance paid for war service, or for service in H.M. Forces, or for a war injury as a civilian. Your rate of benefit may be reduced or, exceptionally, you may not be entitled to benefit at all if you are receiving certain of these payments. You must also tell the Employment Exchange if the rate of pension or allowance changes.

3. **Meaning of "Unemployed."** The general rule is that you must not declare yourself to be unemployed on any day on which you are following any gainful occupation. The only exception to this is when both the following requirements are satisfied :—

(1) The occupation must be one which could ordinarily have been followed by you in addition to your usual employment and outside the ordinary hours of your usual employment ; and

(2) the earnings must not exceed 2/11 on the day in question, or where they are earned in respect of a period longer than a day, must not exceed 6/8d on the daily average.

Whenever you attend the Employment Exchange, tell the clerk if you have done ANY work since your last attendance, even though it may be work which falls within the definition given above. Do not wait for him to ask. Tell him what wages you earned or profit you made whilst working.

4. **Payments from Employers.** Even though you are doing no work, you are not regarded as unemployed on any day for which you are paid by an employer full or part wages or, in certain circumstances, compensation for the loss of your remuneration. Tell the Employment Exchange of any such payment you receive (or have received in recent months) including payment in lieu of notice or a holiday payment.

5. **Night Workers.** When a shift extends through the night, so that work is done both before and after midnight, there are special rules for deciding whether the first or second day can be treated as a day of unemployment.

If you have been on night work, tell the clerk at the Employment Exchange before signing the Register.

6. **Age Limits.** Be sure to state your age correctly. If you are under 18 years of age your rate of benefit may be lower.

When you have reached age 65 (60 for a woman), you may still claim unemployment benefit up to age 70 (65 for a woman) if you do not retire, but only if you would be entitled to a retirement pension if you did retire. After age 70 (65 for a woman) you will have no further right to unemployment benefit.

Tell the Employment Exchange at once if you are not sure what your age is or if you have applied for a retirement pension.

7. **Women Claimants.** The rates of benefit for married women are generally lower than for single women, so you must tell the Employment Exchange at once if you get married while you are claiming benefit.

A married woman aged 18 or over, who is entitled to dependants benefit for her husband, or who is living apart from her husband and cannot get any financial help from him, is entitled to the same rate of benefit as a single woman. A married woman under 18 may be entitled to a higher rate of benefit if she has any dependants, or if she is living apart from her husband and cannot get any financial help from him. If you think you are entitled to benefit at a higher rate, enquire at the Employment Exchange.

If you are drawing a higher rate of benefit and a change in your circumstances occurs, for example, if you no longer have a dependant, you must tell the Employment Exchange immediately. Never represent that you are unmarried if in fact you are a married woman.

NOTE : BENEFIT DUE MUST BE COLLECTED WITHIN SIX MONTHS OF THE DATE WHEN IT IS PAYABLE.

U.I.L. 18

8. **Dependent children.** You may claim increase of benefit for each child in your family under school leaving age, and for any child over school leaving age if under full-time instruction at school or an apprentice, up to but not including 1st August following the 16th birthday. If you are a married woman, living with your husband but claiming on your own insurance, you may claim for children only if your husband is incapable of work. **Tell the Employment Exchange when a child leaves school, or you cease to receive a Family Allowance for any child, or there is any other change of circumstances.**

9. **Dependent Adults.** You may claim for ONE dependent adult only, who must fall into one of the following classes:—

A. Wife or Husband.

(1) A man may claim for his lawful wife, if she is residing with him; or, if they reside apart, provided that he is wholly or mainly maintaining her.

(2) A woman may claim for her lawful husband, if she is wholly or mainly maintaining him and he is incapable of self-support.

B. Close Relative.

You may claim for ONE of the following adult relatives if he or she resides with you and is wholly or mainly maintained by you:—

(1) Father, step-father, grandfather, great grandfather, son, step-son, grandson, great grandson, brother, step brother, half-brother, **if he is incapable of self-support.**

(2) Mother, step-mother, grandmother, great grandmother, daughter, step-daughter, granddaughter, great granddaughter, sister, step-sister, half-sister, provided that, **if she is married, either her husband is incapable of self-support, or she is not residing with him and cannot get financial help from him.**

This includes relatives by adoption.

C. Housekeeper.

(1) You may claim for a housekeeper residing with and wholly or mainly maintained by you, if she has the care of your children and you are entitled to an increase of benefit for a child.

(2) You may claim for a woman who assists in the care of your children, even if she does not reside with you, if you pay her not less than 25/- a week, provided that:—

(a) you employed someone to care for the children before you became unemployed (unless the necessity for employing her did not arise until after you became unemployed); and

(b) you continued to employ someone (not necessarily the same person) after you became unemployed; and

(c) you are entitled to an increase of benefit for a child.

10. **Maintenance.** Where it is necessary for you to show that you are wholly or mainly maintaining the dependant, you will be asked to declare how much a week you pay for maintenance and what other means of support your dependant has, including any contributions made by other members of the household in which your dependant lives.

11. **Dependants Working.** An increase of benefit will not be payable for a wife, a female relative, or a resident housekeeper if she is earning more than 20s. a week, or for a woman who looks after your children and does not live with you if she is earning more than 30s. a week outside her employment with you.

12. **Dependants receiving Other Benefit.** An increase of benefit is normally not payable for a dependant for whom any pension, benefit or allowance is being paid under the National Insurance or Industrial Injuries schemes, or a Government Training Scheme, or for whom a disability pension or allowance is being paid for war service, or service in H.M. Forces, or for war injury as a civilian. In some circumstances, however, an increase of benefit at a reduced rate may be payable in addition to another pension, benefit or allowance.

You must tell the Employment Exchange if and as soon as any payments from any of these sources are claimed, or made to, or in respect of, your dependant, and you must also report if the rate of any benefit, pension or allowance changes.

13. **Dependants residing abroad.** An increase of benefit is not payable for an adult dependant who is abroad, i.e., outside Great Britain, Northern Ireland, and the Isle of Man, except when the dependant resides in one of certain countries with which reciprocal arrangements exist. You should notify the Employment Exchange at once if your wife, husband or any other adult dependant goes abroad.

Subject to the ordinary provisions (e.g., maintenance), an increase for a child who is ordinarily resident in Great Britain will not be affected while he is in another country, provided he is under 15 years of age and the absence is for less than 6 months at a time, but it may be affected if he is over 15 or the absence is for more than 6 months. You should notify the Employment Exchange at once if any of your children goes outside Great Britain.

14. **Change of circumstances.** When you claim for a dependant you will be required to declare on each receipt for unemployment benefit that the conditions for receipt of an increase of benefit are satisfied. Be sure therefore to report any change of circumstances occurring after your claim has been made for example, if your wife obtains work, or qualifies for any of the benefits mentioned in paragraph 12.

ALWAYS GIVE FULL INFORMATION TO THE EMPLOYMENT EXCHANGE, AND BE SURE THAT ANY STATEMENT YOU SIGN IS CORRECT. ANY FALSE REPRESENTATION KNOWINGLY MADE FOR THE PURPOSE OF OBTAINING BENEFIT IS PUNISHABLE ON CONVICTION BY A FINE NOT EXCEEDING £100 OR A TERM OF IMPRISONMENT NOT EXCEEDING THREE MONTHS OR BOTH.

U.I.L. 18

John remained in the UK until 18th December 1948, when he was posted to West Africa, Nigeria. He remained there until 11th November 1949 when he was posted back to England.

In the early 1950s, he moved around several battalions in the UK until on the 1st August 1953, when he was posted to BAOR, Lübbecke, Germany. He, like me, was totally unaware that this posting would have a significant effect on him and his future life. Little did he know when he boarded the ship in Harwich bound for the Hook of Holland that he was heading straight towards the arms of his future wife.

Chapter 15

Although John never spoke of his own family, he spoke very fondly of the relations of Alice. Alice had a sister, Nell (short for some reason for Ellen). Nell was married to Wally (short for Walter) Maycock and they had one child, a daughter, Poppy.

Poppy was christened Ellen but, on the day, she was born, she had lovely rosy cheeks and Wally commented that they were like Poppies and so she became Poppy. Everyone knew her as Poppy for all her life and few people had any idea that it was not her actual name. Apparently, she also signed cheques as Poppy.

Poppy was married to George Davy. Wally and Nell were friends with George's parents and basically, the two were introduced as teenagers and were given little choice but to marry.

Poppy on her wedding day April 1938 – she was 21 years old

John explained that it was a marriage of convenience. He doubted that there was ever much love between them, simply fond affection. Poppy was independent and although she had gone along with her parents' wishes, she had claimed to John that the marriage was never consummated and, consequently, Poppy and George never had children.

I discovered many years later that Poppy had several men 'friends' throughout her life. Whether there was more to these friendships than just being good friends I have no idea. She was a good-looking and smart woman, so it was not a surprise that men were attracted to her.

John was uncle to Poppy through his marriage to Alice who was her aunt and sister to Nell, though she never called him Uncle John. But they were all remarkably close and he obviously adored Poppy, and she him. John on many occasions said that he wanted us to meet as he knew we would all get on.

Over the coming months, John and I became closer and closer. I could not imagine my life without this special and wonderful man. Nothing was ever too much for him where me and little Marietta were concerned. He would go out of his way to ensure that we were cared for and loved unconditionally.

Thankfully, immediately following John contacting Alice with a view to divorcing, she straight away agreed without contest. Alice acknowledged that she was the co-respondent having committed adultery with Ernie. The proceedings commenced, though as already mentioned, we were fully aware that it would be a long process. Once a court date had been established, it would mean that John would need to go back to the UK for the hearing as, in those days, all sides had to appear in court before the judge.

He had agreed with Poppy and George that he would stay with them. Poppy, George, Wally and Nell all lived together in a three-bedroom end of terrace house in Erith in Kent.

Erith is around 25 km from Central London and lies on the south bank of the River Thames. Engineering was an important industry around Erith, with armaments and cables being the main products. During the First World War, Erith was an important area for the manufacture of guns and ammunition. The town suffered heavy bomb damage in the Second World War, mainly due to its position on the riverside near the Royal Arsenal at Woolwich which was only a few miles upriver towards London.

The house was originally just for Nell and Wally but, sadly, Nell had a bad stroke resulting in partial paralysis. Poppy and George agreed to sell their own house and move back with Nell and Wally, and Poppy basically became the carer. This must have been quite a decision for Poppy. She was a fiercely independent woman but felt she had no choice but to give up a career that she thoroughly enjoyed. She was a model dresser and worked for a London fashion house. She would travel by train each day from Erith Station to Central London. So, to give up a job she loved could not have been easy. But she needed to be home and look after Nell – that was paramount. She later found part-time administration work that she could do at home, which was not well paid or interesting, but at least gave her some respite from caring for Nell and Wally.

In those days families often lived close to one another. As it happened, Wally's sister, May, lived next door to them. May and her husband Jack had lived there for many years and the two families were close, often popping in and out of each other's homes.

John meticulously described the house on Collindale Avenue where Poppy, George, Nell and Wally lived. The road consisted of perhaps 100+ houses being either semi-detached, or in groups of three, along terraces on both sides of the road. At one end, adjacent to Hengist Road, there was a corner shop which was known as the top shop, though John said that the road was not on a hill, so he had no explanation. He described it like an Aladdin's Cave. Although small, 'stuff' was crammed in everywhere. You could buy virtually everything you needed from this one small shop: bread, butter, cheese, bacon, sausages, biscuits (cheaper if broken), tea, coffee, sugar, flour, condiments, cleaning goods, brooms, dustpan & brush, cloths, washing lines – everything.

These kinds of shops were a vital component of the local community. The shopkeeper knew all his regular customers by name i.e., Mr or Mrs Davy in the case of Poppy and George. Rarely were first names used – it would be disrespectful. The relationship between a shopkeeper and his customers was special and invariably relied on trust. Often goods were had on 'tick', meaning they were paid for at a later date, usually after payday. Goods purchased were noted in a book and, at the end of a short period, paid for in full. Poppy apparently used this service. She also told the shopkeeper about John so when he visited, he too could buy goods on tick. Goods would sometimes get delivered if needed be. Never at an additional cost; simple good customer service.

At the opposite end of Collindale Avenue was a T-junction with Carlton Road. To the left lead to the 'rec' which were playing fields where all the local kids would congregate for a game of football, hide and seek, cowboys and

Indians, leapfrog, marbles, cricket, etc. To the right of Collindale Avenue, and at the end of Carlton Road was Our Lady of Angels Catholic Church and School.

The Davy's house was about halfway along the road, on the left moving up from Hengist Road. It was on the left end of a block of three houses and of a reasonable size. Downstairs there was a long room as a lounge/dining room. This used to be two separate rooms, but Wally had knocked down the adjoining wall before WW2 to give them a lovely big lounge and dining area.

The kitchen was tiny – long and slim. But from what John said, Poppy was extremely organised and, although only a small area, everything had its place and she was able to produce the most wonderful meals. At the end of the kitchen was a small glazed area, known as a lean-to, where there was a twin tub washing machine and storage cupboards. Then the back door to the garden. The garden was long and thin. There were bordered areas both sides, but the middle was mostly paved with potted plants here and there. Again, John said this was Poppy's doing as she wanted to make everything as easy to manage as possible and provide a nice flat area so Nell could get outside if she wanted to.

At the end of the garden was a garage but it was mostly used for storage rather than for a car. George had a car which he parked on the street outside the front of the house.

Upstairs were three bedrooms. One, fairly large, that Poppy and George used, which faced the front of the house. Directly next to this was a small room, known as a box room, which had a single bed and John used this when he stayed. This also faced the front of the house. At the back was another double bedroom that Wally and Nell used. Next to their bedroom was the bathroom: bath, loo and sink – no shower in those days. John also mentioned that on the bathroom door was a little ceramic sign which simply said 'yer tis' – short for here it is!

John said that Poppy was always dressed smartly. Maybe this was because of her time working in the fashion industry. She would go to the hairdressers every week, wore make-up, bright red nail polish and dressed immaculately. Never would she leave the house without putting her 'face' on. He so made me smile when he explained that Poppy had a great pair of 'pins' (pin pegs is cockney rhyming slang for legs). She was immensely proud of her legs and he said it did not take much for her to lift up skirt/dress and show them off. I was not sure about this and it did seem somewhat exhibitionist.

Poppy had another love, and that was poodle dogs. She had been keeping the breed for many years. I suppose as Poppy and George had no children the dogs took their place. They were treated like royalty, and everything they could wish for they were indulged with. John so made me laugh when he relayed the story that upon returning from a walk, they had to remain in the lean-to area at the back of the kitchen and wait to be wiped down. This not only included their paws but also their mouths and bottoms too. They had their own cupboard in the lean-to which contained food, treats and their own individual towels, which had been embroidered with their respective names, Sally and Sue. I could not wait to get to England and witness this palaver. It all seemed so extraordinarily extreme to me. But then I was not animal friendly. We never had any animals as I was growing up and I did not see the need for any now... and never have.

All too soon, heartbreak was to beset me again. Mutti had been unwell for a while and I felt helpless being so far away from her. It was not at all easy to get to Berlin. Mutti had been to several hospital appointments and nothing conclusive was diagnosed. But she had told me she had been putting on weight and had no idea why as she was not eating that much.

Then the fateful day arrived, and I received a telephone call at Tax House to tell me that she had died in hospital. This was on 8th April 1955. I now know that what she had was ovarian cancer. In those days there was little that could be done, and the diagnosis was not easy. I told John straight away and he was extremely comforting. He commented that the date also happened to be the birthday of Poppy.

Of course, I immediately planned to travel to Berlin to sort out the funeral and Mutti's possessions. Frau Schmidt agreed to look after little Marietta as it was not appropriate for me to take her with me. Captain Meade understood the situation and I was given immediate compassionate leave. He added that I should take as long as I need and that would not be a problem at all.

I knew that it was going to be a long, arduous and sad journey. I had mixed feelings. It was always wonderful to visit my home city as it was changing almost every week with a massive building program in progress. But this time it was to deal with the death of my beloved mother. Having arrived, of course, I managed everything in my usual efficient manner. The hospital had transferred my mother's body to a funeral parlour. As soon as I arrived, I made my way there to pay my last respects. They were immensely helpful and assisted me in planning for the funeral. We could not afford much so it was to be a simple ceremony, coffin and headstone. Mutti was to be buried alongside my father and brother in Stephanus. So, once again, they were all together.

Her possessions were minimal, and it did not take long to clear her apartment. Neighbours took some bits and pieces, and other lightweight items, paperwork and photos, etc., I packed into a suitcase to take with me back to Lübbecke. The furniture was collected by a charity that took things for those less fortunate. And so that was that. It was heart-breaking in some ways to once again leave and head back to Lübbecke. But also, on my mind were the horrible incidents that I witnessed in Berlin during the war. I never ever wanted to experience anything like that again. I left Berlin not looking back. Mutti, Papa and Gerhard will always be with me in my heart, no matter where in this world I would end up. So many painful memories. I knew that it would be unlikely that I would ever return to Berlin.

Once back in Lübbecke a sense of relief enveloped me. John came to the station to meet me and to my surprise, he had little Marietta with him. Marietta ran at me and gave me such a wonderful hug. John did the same and kissed me intensely. I was home with my family, surrounded by the most wonderful and special love.

G 2

Sterbeurkunde

(Standesamt Kreuzberg von Berlin Nr. 839/1955)

Die Rentenempfängerin Herta Frieda Olga – – –

S c h i l d geborene Rössel – – – – – – – –,

wohnhaft in Berlin-Neukölln,Schöneweider Straße, 23–

ist am 8. April 1955 – – um –16– Uhr –15– Minuten

in Berlin , Mariannenplatz 1 bis 3 – – – – – – – –

– – – – – – – – – – – – – – – – verstorben.

Die Verstorbene war geboren am 26. Januar 1892 – –

in Wartin,Kreis Randow – – – – – – – – – – –

(Standesamt Casekow – – – – – – – – Nr. 10/1892)

Die Verstorbene war nicht verheiratet Witwe von – –

Paul Richard Max Schild. – – – – – – – – –

Berlin – – – – – – – – , den 12. April 195 5 .

Der Standesbeamte
In Vertretung

Klemmt

Ka.

DM 1.-

rbeurkunde G 2
Mai. 1955   Din A 6. 50 000. 2. 55 (P)

Herta Schild death certificate 8th April 1955

Chapter 16

John and I had by this time become remarkably close and much in love. In August 1955, we decided we both needed a break so arranged to have a holiday to Bavaria to give us both respite from the day-to-day routine, and to help me get over missing Mutti so very much. Little Marietta stayed with Frau and Herr Schmidt, and, after we had dropped her off with them, John and I travelled by train to Konstanz.

Konstanz (Constance in English) is situated on Lake Bodensee and the River Rhine passes through the lake. Because it almost lies within Switzerland, directly adjacent to the Swiss border, Konstanz was not bombed by the Allied Forces during World War II. The city left all its lights on at night, and thus fooled the bombers into thinking it was actually part of Switzerland. Therefore, the town had all its beautiful old buildings intact.

The holiday was incredibly special. It gave us time alone and time to really get to know each other. Of course, we were both much in love at this stage of our relationship and simply never, ever wanted to be parted.

John being John, and his love of writing, he sent a postcard each day to Poppy to let her know we were well and thoroughly enjoying our time away.

As it happens, I have all these postcards. Poppy had kept them and years later she gave them to me. They are in a pretty poor state as unfortunately, her house sustained bad fire damage in the late 1960s and the postcards were badly scorched.

As well as John writing each day to Poppy, he also took many photographs and bought several scenic postcards. When we got back to Lubbecke, he bought an album and then carefully stuck them all in it. The pages of the album are black and so John used a white pen to put notes under each photograph to explain where it had been taken. I still have this album – so many happy memories. It was so lovely to travel around this area of so much natural beauty.

Train tickets from Switzerland holiday August 1955

The next few months passed by quickly and, surprisingly promptly, the time came when John would travel back to England. I did not want him to leave us, but I knew it was a means to an end. Soon he would be back with us again and, all being well, divorced, so we could marry, and that time could not come around quickly enough for us both. We hated being apart. Since we met, now some two years ago, we had always been together. I could not imagine life without my wonderful special loving soldier.

His journey began on Friday 28th October 1955, and was reasonably good. He took a local train first to Minden mid-morning and then left Minden at 12:20 by train which made its way to the Hook of Holland. There he got the ferry to Harwich. John being John, immediately found the bar on board to have a few drinks and supper and whilst there met several men from the RAF (Royal Air Force). He had no idea what time the ship sailed, but he thought around 10 pm. By this time, he was tired and made for his bed. He did not wake again until they berthed in the morning at Harwich.

They disembarked around 7 am and then it was back on to a train to Liverpool Street Station in Central London. He journeyed up to London with the RAF fellows he had met in Holland. Having arrived in London at around 10:30 am they went for a cuppa together, then said their goodbyes and parted company. John rang Poppy to let her know he had arrived. It had been arranged that John would meet George at Charing Cross Station and they would then both go and see the Arsenal play, who were John's favourite football team.

The Arsenal Football Club was founded in 1886 as a munition workers' team from Woolwich, then in Kent, now Southeast London. They turned professional in 1891 and joined The Football League two years later. They were promoted to the First Division in 1904, but financial problems meant they were liquidated and reformed. They were bought out by Sir Henry Norris that year and to improve the club's financial standing, he moved the team to the Arsenal Stadium, Highbury, North London in 1913.

The name of the team came from the Royal Arsenal, Woolwich which carried out armaments manufacture, ammunition proofing and explosives research for the British armed forces at a site on the south bank of the River Thames. It was originally known as the Woolwich Warren, having begun on land previously used as a domestic warren in the grounds of a Tudor house, Tower Place. Much of the initial history of the site is linked with that of the Board of Ordnance, which purchased the Warren in the late 17th century in order to expand an earlier base at Gun Wharf in Woolwich Dockyard.

Over the next two centuries, as operations grew and innovations were pursued, the site expanded massively; at the time of the First World War, the Arsenal covered 1,285 acres (520 ha) and employed close to 80,000 people.

It was to Highbury, near Islington in North London, that George and John went on bus number 4, to watch the match. Sadly, Arsenal lost the game but, despite this, he thoroughly enjoyed watching the match. He said that once he got me to England, he would take me to a match. I have to say I was not that impressed. Of course, I would support him and his team, but I did not think I would want to go to a stadium to watch them. And I never did. After the football match, they made their way to Erith.

John fully expected that Nell would be sat by the window watching the road awaiting their arrival. And that was the case because, as soon as he rang the doorbell, she was already up and waiting for him to come into the lounge. She straight away gave him a warm Erith welcome as he put it, which was a big hug.

Her first question was how I and little Marietta were. John had been writing to Poppy on a regular basis and they knew all about us. They could not wait to meet us. This was so incredibly pleasing for me.

One other thing that was mentioned was that I should be teaching little Marietta some English. They wanted to ensure that when we finally got over to England that little Marietta would be able to manage some basic English. Of course, that was my intention to, and we had already started.

Each day, John's letters would arrive. Each one began and finished differently: *Erika my dearest sweetheart* and ending *God bless your darling, your ardent lover, John.*

Erika my darling and ever yours.
Erika my sweetheart and darling and God bless you my darling, I am ever yours. Erika, darling of mine and I am forever your ardent lover.

As already said the words were so incredibly special. Falling in love with this man was amazingly easy. We had both agreed to write to one another every day though sometimes the postal service made life difficult for us. Often letters would arrive in a different order than which they were sent. My letters to John, I sent directly to Collindale Avenue. John's letters to me though were not delivered to my home. Instead, I had to walk to the post office each day and see whether there was anything for me. On one occasion, I went to the post office to collect the letter(s) and when I did, I noticed that one had already been opened. This annoyed me greatly and I complained. It transpired that my landlord had 'inadvertently' opened my letter by mistake. As the letters are clearly addressed to me, I was incredibly angry, to say the least. I think he was just being nosey.

Each day, like John, I tried to write three of four pages. Most days though there was not a lot of news to tell him. Generally, it was describing the day-to-day events, getting up, work, shopping, dinner, sleeping, etc.

Whilst John was in England, I decided to take little Marietta to Bremen for a day out and shopping to help take my mind off missing him so much. It was a treat for her as she loved to go on a train and got overly excited. I did have friends in Bremen, well on the outskirts of the city, but our trip was only for the day so unfortunately on this occasion we would not be able to meet them. My primary reason for going there was that the shops were much better than in Lübbecke.

I wanted to buy some new clothes and some presents for my American friends. It was a shame that John was not with me as I would have liked to have had his opinion on the clothes I purchased. I just hoped that he liked them. I was still dressmaking, but it was rather nice, if I could afford it, to buy something from a shop. My friends in America meant so much to me. Although we were akin to strangers, they helped us so significantly after WW2 and now it was my turn to reciprocate in a small way.

Marietta was now married to Bill Ekberg and by 1955, they had three girls, Judy, Nancy, & Marietta (known as Mary). Little Marietta helped me choose a few small toys for the girls. We had such fun playing with them before deciding what to buy. One of the toys was a poodle dog which was almost too beautiful to play with. It was wonderful to spend such quality time with little Marietta. She was truly a beautiful child with such a lovely countenance.

In addition to the poodle, I bought some special chocolates and fruits made from marzipan. The fruits were incredible and certainly looked like the real thing. I was positive that my American friends would love the gesture and be so pleased to receive a parcel of so many lovely things.

Philip (PJ) and Etta Meyer

Marietta and Bill Ekberg with first born, Judy

The Ekberg's – Bill, Marietta, Grandmother Etta, Judy, Peggy, Mary, Nancy and Susie
– taken in 1965

113

Chapter 17

I was so lonely without John around. Little Marietta and I would often go around to Frau and Herr Schmidt. They were such good friends to us. They adored little Marietta and she them. Often, Herr Schmidt would sit little Marietta on his lap and read fairy stories to her for hours. She absolutely loved this and was totally enthralled. He would change his voice to suit the characters in the story and this very much brought the stories alive.

Our day-to-day routine was much the same. Although John was away, we would still go for a lovely long walk on Sundays. As already mentioned, the countryside around us was beautiful and thankfully we were a small part of rural Germany that was not devastated from WW2. Little Marietta loved our walks and liked to pick wildflowers to bring home and if she saw a butterfly she would instantly chase after it. She had absolutely no intention of catching it but simply enjoying the chase.

We had decided to have a holiday together in England in May 1956 and, of course, little Marietta would be with us. All being well, if the divorce remained uncontested then we would be arranging our wedding at the same time.

Whilst John stayed with the Davy's, he was certainly well looked after. John was forever telling me what a wonderful cook Poppy was and that she made him so many lovely meals. He did though always compliment me on my cooking as well. I tried to cook English meals for John as I know he enjoyed them – a good roast for instance. Practice makes perfect he would say to me. As well as lovely dinners, Poppy also cooked John breakfast most days. He was so funny as he would assure me that although he had put on a few pounds it was not much and it would soon be off again. Even in his letters, he would so make me laugh. He had the most glorious sense of humour.

He always said things for me to tell Little Marietta. Obviously, he sent his love to her but in one letter he asked me to tell her that she needed to save up her pfennigs as she would have to pay her own fare to England for our holiday. So, naughty of him. Little Marietta made me smile when I relayed John's sentiments from his last letter to her. Her immediate reply was that she had no pfennigs at all and did not know when or where she would get any. But I told her not to worry it was just John being funny. At the time, I was just finishing off my letter in reply to John, and Marietta stared at the last sheet looking rather puzzled. Bless her, she then asked what all the crosses meant at the end of the letter. It was so very sweet. Of course, I said they were kisses; an indication of our love for one another.

John enjoyed going to the cinema and he would go whenever he could. It was a past-time that he thoroughly relished. Often, he would take Nell with him as she loved the movies as much as he did. Each letter that I received contained news and detailing everything he had done on the day. I do not know how he always thought of so much to tell me, but he did; each and every day.

In one letter he went into detail about going to Woolwich which had a particularly good shopping centre and buying a new hat. He decided to not buy an inexpensive hat as it would have to be packed to travel back to Germany. He told me that the hat cost 22/6d equivalent at the time to around 11 Marks and would be good for knocking around in. When settled, he intended to buy a much better-quality hat. John, as I have said before, was always extremely smart whether in uniform or in civvies and he invariably always wore a hat.

The weeks passed by and finally came the day, being Monday 7th November 1955, when John was due to travel to London and the court for the divorce hearing. He sent me a telegram with the fantastic news that his divorce had been granted by simply saying 'all OK today' but also a longer letter followed in which he gave more details.

Telegram from John confirming divorce 7th November 1955

On the day of the hearing, he had travelled up to London from Erith by train early in the morning and was really keyed up, quite ill in fact, and felt the same as he entered the courtroom. There were a couple of other cases before his so he could see what the procedure was and gradually he began to settle down and waited. Slowly but surely becoming quite composed. The proceedings for his case took around 35 minutes in all, which was somewhat quicker than he had expected. His counsel was exceptionally good with brains and fortitude which certainly won the day for him, though of course, it was John's from the start. There was a debate about costs and the judge ruled that they should be shared so he would get a refund and he was happy about that.

He then went on to say that finally, we will be in a position to carry out our plans for the future. It meant that we would soon be able to announce to the world at large that we were entitled to love each other forever and ever and that he loves me so very much and that I, his sweetheart, should never think otherwise. He felt as though he was in paradise and had never dreamt that he would ever feel the way that he does. He loved me unconditionally forever and ever. Two more weeks and we will be together again to start of life of heavenly bliss. He wanted us to get officially engaged on 1st January 1956.

John continued to write to me every day. Always detailing the events of the day. The routine was reasonably similar each day. George would go off to work in London during the week but at the weekends they would spend time together. If a new film came out, then they went to the picture house. There was a small picture house in Erith, but they would sometime travel by bus to the neighbouring town of Bexleyheath which had a large ABC theatre.

The letter I received written on the 14th of November 1955 was rather prophetic, though at the time, obviously, I had no idea what would transpire. We often discussed the road ahead that we would be travelling together. He said that he knew it would be hard for us to keep our love as there are always many pitfalls along the way to be circumvented. But he was certain that between us we would be able to overcome any difficulties that came our way. We would forever be our two selves plus of course forever darling little Marietta who would make our family complete. Of course, should any other Crowleys come to hand, well, he guessed we would manage.

He also suggested that we should arrange a small party on the occasion of our engagement as, after all, he wanted to broadcast to the whole world how much we love each other. Nothing on a grand scale but maybe someone in quarters would have an idea of a venue to use or maybe we could use the local Hoff.

On Wednesday 16th November 1955, George drove John to Canterbury to visit Athelstan Road and pick up the last of his possessions. Thankfully, everything was amicable between John and Alice, so it was a simple formality. Alice and Ernie had packed up John's possessions and left them in the attic for as and when he could collect them. He said that he was pleased to have completely severed all connections with the place that had so many bad memories for him and never would he ever have cause to visit there again.

One thing that he brought back was a lamp standard that Wally had been after for years. He described it as a good piece of furniture but thought that I would probably not like it so much because it was a nude woman. He went on to explain that it was a thing of beauty and carved from a piece of ebony wood. It stood around 50 cm high, was incredibly heavy and also quite unusual. When he got back to Erith with it, Wally was overjoyed. John had bought it in Nigeria when stationed there in 1948.

There was also a small letter opener, again from Nigeria. This had a tribal woman's head at the top and this tapered down about six inches in the form of a body with a sharp point at the bottom. I have never used it as a letter opener but simply as a decoration and it hangs on a hook in my lounge.

Nigerian carved ebony lamp standard

Finally, the 20th of November 1955 arrived, and John began his journey back to me as a single man. George drove him to Liverpool Street Station in London to get the train to Harwich. He arrived at Harwich at 10 pm and immediately boarded the ship. The sailing was straightforward with no issue. He arrived home in Lange Straße on Monday evening at around 8:30 pm. It was so incredibly wonderful to have him home again. I had missed him so much. Little Marietta had wanted to stay up and wait for him, but I managed to persuade her to go to bed at 7 pm and told her I had no idea when John would arrive. We had supper together and then went straight to bed as, bless him, he was absolutely shattered from the journey.

So, on this wonderful night, we began to make plans to spend the rest of our lives together. I could not have wanted anything more. John was incredibly special, and so much so, that it hurt being apart. He was truly remarkable. Our love knew no bounds. We were together, forever.

John and Alice – divorce certificate

Chapter 18

John announced our engagement to his army buddies, and they were all pleased for us. He explained that all we wanted was a small get together and nothing fancy. We thought about a number of places to have our party and, in the end, arranged a private room in the local Hoff. John had invited a few of his army pals and I invited a few of my friends. All in all, we were a group of around twelve, which was perfect.

We were not expecting any presents but the lads in the officers' mess had arranged a collection and bought us a beautiful musical stein together with a Japanese tea service as a joint engagement and wedding present. The tea service was rather special as it had lithopone of geisha girls on the base of the cups. It is quite beautiful. We all had a wonderful time and probably drank far too much but then we were celebrating, so no harm done.

Japanese tea service – present from officers' mess, Lübbecke

Musical stein – present from officers' mess, Lübbecke

It was necessary for John to get permission from his commanding officer that we could marry. Without doing so, it could be deemed as a breach of discipline. Directly after WW2, the British Army would not allow marriage between serving soldiers and German nationals. In 1946 it eased, but even in 1956 marriage between British Army personnel and German citizens was still frowned upon. Thankfully, this first hurdle went without issue and permission to marry was granted. I suppose it helped that they knew me well having worked at Tax House for a couple of years.

Letter granting permission for John and Erika to marry

John and I had discussed at length as to where we would live once married and whether he should remain in the army. He had been considering his future for some significant time. He absolutely loved the routine of army life and had known nothing else. He was now in his 33rd year of service and decided that the time had come when he would call it a day. The change would be huge, but he said absolutely worth it as he would be able to spend much more time with me and little Marietta and he truly did not want to be parted from us for any length of time.

Money was always an issue. We had little and would definitely need a small sum in order to move along with our plans. Therefore, going forward we would have to save and save and save. Every penny/pfennig had to be carefully considered as to whether it should be spent. Once again, I took up dressmaking and knitting to earn a little bit more. John restricted himself from going to the bar for more than one pint. He found that extremely hard but was more than willing to make the sacrifice.

John wanted us to move to England. I was not so sure about this at first as it would be a huge upheaval for me and I was also worried about how the English would treat me and little Marietta. The next concern was what job John could do. He had known nothing but the army and in recent years had a desk job. Therefore, he thought that perhaps he could do security or caretaking or something along those lines.

Little Marietta was only nine years old in 1956, and she would not only be leaving her home country but moving to a foreign land, speaking a different language, attending an English school and needed to integrate into a society where undoubtedly the recent memories of WW2 would definitely be a factor. John continually reassured me but deep down inside I was so incredibly worried.

The next mammoth task was arranging the wedding and the implications that it would undoubtedly cause. John wanted to marry in England, in Erith with Poppy and her family with us. This was especially important to him. Obtaining the necessary paperwork for me was relatively easy and that surprised me. I had assumed that there would be a huge amount of bureaucracy but actually, everything went along quite smoothly.

We would journey to England in May 1956, planned to marry in June. John got in touch with Poppy and she kindly went to the local registry office to find out exactly what was needed and dates available in June. She sent us a telegram to let us know that she had booked for 11 am on Saturday 2nd June 1956. All the other details she put into a letter. We knew the following months would pass by very quickly and they did.

As mentioned, we were saving as much as possible and so when my birthday in February arrived, it came and went without much celebration. But, when John's birthday came around on 19th April, we decided to at least have a few drinks in the officers' mess, which we did and thoroughly enjoyed. John came back to my flat and more often than not he would spend the night with me.

It had taken John a long time to get into my bed. As much as I loved him, I did not think it appropriate for quite a long while after we first met that we should sleep together whilst he was still married to Alice. He was incredibly patient with me. Many other men would probably have disappeared. But he was there for the duration and had absolutely no intention of going anywhere. So, he continued to 'woo' me until finally, I surrendered. I loved this man so much and making love with him was a natural progression of our relationship. As with everything else with John, he was ever the gentleman in every respect. Once I accepted his sexual advances, we enjoyed the most wonderfully fulfilling sex life.

Before we knew it, May had arrived. Soon we would be travelling to England to get married. After our holiday was over, we would be travelling back to Germany again but this time as Mr and Mrs Crowley. There was not enough room for us to stay with Poppy and George, so Poppy had arranged rooms for us in a local pub called The Red Barn. It was only a short distance from them, and she was sure it would suit us. Plus, it was not as expensive as a hotel would be and that was crucial as money was, and continued to be, tight.

As with John's previous journey to England, we set off by train to Hook of Holland, ferry to Harwich and then train to Liverpool Street Station in London. Little Marietta was both excited and scared about her first trip to England. And to be honest, so was I. We had one large suitcase together with a smaller one. John had left a few things at Poppy's, so he did not need to bring that much with him. As the train drew into Liverpool Street I began to physically shake with apprehension. John gave me a hug and said I should not worry. It had been arranged that George would meet us at Liverpool Street Station.

We alighted the train and made our way along the platform to the barrier. As we approached it, I could see a tall slim man with dark hair waving. John said straight away that this was George. Having given our tickets over, we walked through the gate. George greeted us like long lost friends and made me and little Marietta feel so welcomed. Little Marietta even managed to say hello and thanked George for coming to meet us in the most wonderful English. She also called him Uncle George which I think he especially liked as he was beaming from ear to ear. He helped John with the luggage and then showed us where he had parked the car which was only a short walk away.

Little Marietta clung on to me so tightly as we walked through the station. She hardly said another word. Once the luggage was stored in the boot, we all got in the car; George and John in the front and me and little Marietta in the back.

Slowly we made our way from Liverpool Street Station, along Bishopsgate towards London Bridge. John was extremely excited at being able to describe our journey to us and telling us the names of the roads, bridges, etc. and pointing our places of interest. Having crossed over London Bridge, we made for the Elephant and Castle, then on to the Old Kent Road towards New Cross and

Blackheath. Once we had gone over the heath, we travelled down Shooters Hill on to Welling, then turned left towards Erith.

The journey took us about an hour and a half, but the time passed quickly.

John has so meticulously described Collindale Avenue to me that as soon as we turned into the road, I seemed to instantly recognise it. We pulled up outside number 50 and, virtually immediately, there on the step to greet us was Poppy. Her arms were wide opened, and she gave me the most wonderful hug and said how excited she was to finally meet me and little Marietta. Instantly we were ushered inside to meet Nell and Wally.

Poppy had prepared a light supper for us as she knew we would be tired from our journey and keen to get to the pub and our beds. It was so wonderful to be greeted with such warmth. Out first meeting could not have gone any better. I knew instantly that I would love Poppy and her family as much as my dear John did.

All too soon, it was time for us to depart again and head for The Red Barn. But we would be back again the next morning as Poppy had all sorts of things planned for us.

Prior to the actual wedding day, we spent a great deal of time with Poppy and her family. As John had assured me, they were perfectly wonderful to me and little Marietta. By this time, little Marietta had learned quite a bit of English, so could hold a basic conversation with everyone and they were so pleased. It must have been so awfully hard for her but she coped admirably. John took me Woolwich and to Bexleyheath to do some shopping. We had set aside a little money to buy a few small gifts for Poppy and George, as they had been so truly kind to us.

Chapter 19

Our wedding day arrived on, Saturday 2nd June 1956.

Poppy had arranged for me to have my hair done first thing in the morning as she obviously knew I would want to look my best. She had also arranged with a local florist that we should each have beautiful wedding buttonholes, mine being a carnation and John's a large white gardenia. Both our suits were pressed to perfection, as was the lovely dress that little Marietta wore.

The day of the wedding was wonderful. The weather was kind to us, and the sun shone all day long. The ceremony itself in the local registry office was simple – John said his piece and I said mine and that was it. Everything went so well and finally; we were Mr and Mrs John Crowley. Then it was back to Collindale Avenue for a get-together.

We were 12 people in all: John and I and little Marietta; Poppy and George; Nell and Wally; Pat and John (lifelong friends of Poppy); and Wally's sister, May and her husband, Jack, with their daughter, Joyce, joined us. Poppy had been terribly busy and laid on a lovely buffet and we also had the most special wedding cake. We all ate too much and drank too much, but it did not matter.

The wedding party – George, Pat, John, Joyce, Poppy, little Marietta, May, Erika,
Wally, John, Jack and Nell

Telegram received on our wedding day – 2nd July 1956

The happy couple

All too soon, we had to say our goodbyes and get in our taxi back to The Red Barn. George would have driven us to the Red Barn, but he too had been celebrating and it would not have been sensible for him to drive having had quite a bit to drink. It was such a nice end to a perfect day. Come Monday morning, we would again be on our way back to Germany.

I have mentioned that John's letters and some of mine have been kept and stored in a small blue box. Also, within the box of letters are the remains of my corsage from our wedding day. It is now virtually disintegrated and very little left of the bloom, just a stem and a bit of wire and pieces of petals. But then it has been in the box nigh on 60 years!

As you know from what you have already read, John had described Collindale Avenue and the family in great detail. I was also able to witness first-hand the palaver with the dogs, Sally and Sue. They truly were treated like royalty and not like dogs at all. They were sweet though and would try to sit on my lap – but I was not so keen.

John, Poppy, George, Nell and Wally all smoked, which was the thing in those days. It was not something that I particularly liked but I would join in now and again. Heaven knows why, but I suppose just simply not be an outsider. We had no idea about the health consequences in those days.

One other observation from this stay with Poppy and her family was that I was stunned at how incredibly tiny Poppy's feet were. She was around 5ft 6in tall, so not short but she wore only UK size 2-3 shoes. Her feet were minuscule. Seeing her shoes or slippers around the house always made me smile because they looked like children's.

It was time to head back to Germany. It was such an amazing feeling being so much in love with this incredibly special, generous and affectionate man. Life going forward was going to be difficult, as we did not have much, but that did not matter. We were a family: me, little Marietta and John. Plus, I was now quite certain that there would be another Crowley to join us – expected sometime in January 1957.

John was extremely excited when I told him that I believed I was pregnant. He hugged me so tightly, never wanting to let me go. We decided not to say anything at the wedding as, of course, I was pregnant before we married. When we thought back, we could probably name the day precisely when I conceived. It would have been on John's birthday on 19th April. We so laughed about this once we realised the connection. He immediately exclaimed, "What a wonderful birthday present. You couldn't have given me anything more delightful." We would have to wait until sometime in January and, all being well, be delivered an addition to our family. But that was a few months ahead.

Chapter 20

We now had the task of the massive undertaking of John resigning, him finding a new position and then all of us moving to the UK. Followed by, of course, the birth of our baby. So much to organise in such a short time. I knew though that with the enormous amount of love and affection we had between us we would surmount any difficulties put before us and look forward to a new chapter in our lives.

And so, we settled down to married family life in Lübbecke. I was still working at Tax House as was John. Little Marietta was so excited to have a dad at last and cherished every moment that she was with John. He truly adored her and was so good with her. John has resigned but did not initially have an actual leave date. It was expected that he would have to travel to the UK and have his final days there.

RAPC Lübbecke 1956

My pregnancy was going well and without any problems. Being that I was still employed by the British Army, they looked after prenatal care and I could not have asked for better support and help. Little Marietta was extremely excited about having a brother or sister and it could not happen quick enough for her. Virtually every day she would ask me was her sibling going to arrive today, and I would patiently tell her no, not for a few months. But regardless, she still continued to ask.

John was finally advised that he was being posted back to the UK to finish his time there. He also had leave that he was entitled to and would take that at the same time. Unexpectedly, when his orders came through, he had to leave virtually immediately. On 20th October 1956, he began the journey back to the UK. The usual route of a train to Hook of Holland, then the ferry to Harwich and a train again to Liverpool Street Station in Central London. Poppy, of course, had arranged for George to meet him at Liverpool Street Station. So, at least he would not have to get another train and could have the comfort of being driven to Collindale Avenue.

John left Lübbecke abruptly. Not intentionally but simply because the arrangements came through to transfer to the UK last minute, so he had no choice but to pack and ship out very quickly. Of course, the next letter I received was full of remorse. He first said how deeply sorry he was that he was not able to say goodbye to little Marietta and that worried him greatly. He was so concerned that she would be upset. I had explained to little Marietta that this was unintentional, simply that his orders came through the last minute, so he just had to go immediately.

It was awful for me too, seeing John leave again. I was in the throes of pregnancy blues being now some six months along. I did not want John to go and my eyes were full of tears as he said goodbye. This greatly affected John. He did not know how to handle the situation and so, hastily, turned, went out of the door and disappeared down the road. Also, in this letter, he reassured me of his unconditional love and that he was counting the days to when we could be together again. It would not be long, only a few weeks. But those days felt like a lifetime. The good news was that John had an interview with a brewery with the possibility of a job in the pub we had stayed at just before we married. This had been arranged via Pat and John who were friends of Poppy and George and had attended our wedding.

He was also on the hunt for accommodation and that was proving a rather difficult task. Every time he found something, by the time he called, it was already taken. But, if push came to shove, as long as he could find somewhere for me and Marietta, he could for the time being stay in quarters.

In his next letter, John advised that the manager of the Red Barn had offered him a position but was disappointed that he would not be able to start straight away. But at least there was a job for him, and he was happy to wait for a few weeks. He also said that he had to call RAPC Foots Cray and was disappointed that they knew nothing of him or his situation. He fully explained everything. Then half an hour later he had a return call demanding that he immediately report for duty. He calmly advised that he was on leave so that to attend immediately was not possible.

I could no longer work but thankfully, I was able to sign on at the labour exchange and received 39.60 Marks a week and that really helped. John had left me some money, so little Marietta and I were able to manage. We had explained at length to little Marietta what would be happening in the near future and, not unexpectedly, she was worried. Bless her, she was only nine years old and not only moving to a new school but in a new country with a new language to learn. She was reluctant to move away from the town she loved, the school she enjoyed and most importantly, her friends. Of course, I tried to reassure her that she would soon make new friends, but it was nonetheless, extremely daunting for such a little soul.

John departed so quickly that he had left a few things behind that he needed. I packed up what he had asked for and arranged to send them to Collindale Avenue. He had also left behind a pair of flannel trousers. He had mentioned that he had the intention of throwing them away but to me, they still had a lot of life left in them. Therefore, I washed and laundered them and pressed as best I could. The result was passable, and I hoped John would be happy.

Another memory from this time was in relation to the content of a letter from John. As already mentioned, in each letter he would always send his love to me and little Marietta. On this occasion, though, this is what he said: "Please send my love to little Marietta from her beloved 'farter'." He, of course, thought this so incredibly funny by making a play on words for the German word for father being Vater but pronounced like the naughty English word of farter. When I replied to his letter, I made a point of telling him off for using such language. I know he was only joking but I truly felt that there was definitely no need to use such profanity.

On 27th October 1956, John moved out from Poppy and George's and instead went into quarters at The Regimental Pay Office, Foots Cray, Kent. He could have stayed for a bit longer with the Davy's, but it was such a jumble with everyone getting up in the morning at a similar time and getting ready for work with only one bathroom. Therefore, he would remain in barracks for the time being. He also had applied to rent a whole house in Edenbridge, Kent. This would be wonderful but probably unlikely that anything would come of it as everything seems to be going so quickly.

Much of my time was spent packing the final bits and pieces and getting ready for the move to England. I had to be prepared. It was pretty tough though with my bump getting bigger by the day. I became quite tired rather quickly but had to push myself and be organised. Little Willy, as we had named the bump, was quite active in the morning but later in the day settled down. Thankfully, I had no pain as such and hoped everything was all right. My greatest wish was for a healthy baby and I would be the happiest wife in the world if it could be a boy, exactly like his father because I loved him so very much. However, not quite so big, or as thirsty as his father because I was afraid he would drain me!

One important and essential item for me to buy were feather beds (duvets). There was absolutely no way that I would struggle beneath sheets and blankets on our bed in England. I could not fathom why the British thought this bedding arrangement to be practicable. Being restrained underneath tight bedsheets was absolutely not for me. I had planned to buy three feather beds – one each for me and John and one for little Marietta. Why on earth battle and fight over double bed sheets/blankets. Simple German solution – you have your own individual bedding. Perfect.

A new store (Kolck) opposite the mess was due to open imminently, and I made an appointment with Frau Schmidt to go to the store on opening day as we had been assured that there would be lots of good bargains. I hoped to buy the feather beds and some linen and maybe a few other items if money allowed. Thankfully, bargains were to be had and I managed to get three beautiful goose down feather beds along with the necessary sheets and pillowslips. Plus, a couple of tablecloths, towels and, finally, some remnants of material that I thought would do for cushions. All were delivered to the flat, at no additional cost, in preparation of being boxed up and shipped off to England.

Finally, the day came when John finished with the army for good. Our new life ahead was now coming together.

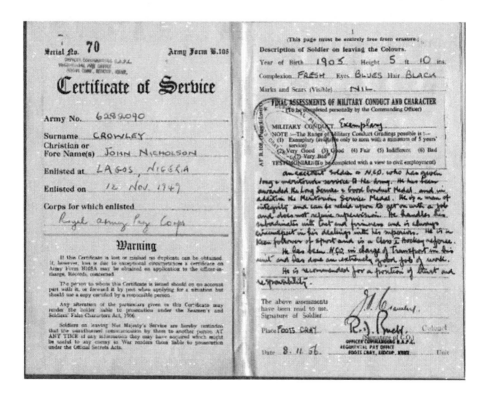

John's paybook updated with a lovely discharge testament

The next letter received came with incredibly exciting news. John had been offered a position as a trainee at The Red Barn and had already moved in. The house in Edenbridge was not to be but, the landlord had agreed that me and little Marietta could join him there as soon as possible. John had also arranged that the furniture and packing cases could be stored for as long as we need with Bonners, in Welling, Kent which was close to Erith and the Red Barn in Barnehurst.

So, all speed ahead now and packing up the last of our things and planning the journey to England. Soon I would be back in the arms of my special and wonderful husband.

However, the next letter contained worrying news. It seemed that the brewery had decided that me and little Marietta could not stay at the pub. All bureaucratic apparently. But John assured me that he had made alternative arrangements and that I should not be concerned as everything would be ready for us when we arrived.

I continued with the packing and reassuring little Marietta that all would be well. She was so still concerned and upset about leaving Germany.

The army had kindly arranged to ship all our furniture and belongings to the UK. I think this was because of John's long 33-year service – it definitely counted for something. Also, he had spent years working in transportation, so everyone knew him and were more than willing to help. The soldiers that arrived to manage the packing could not have been more helpful. Seeing my enormous bump helped I suppose, as they would not let me lift a thing. Everything was done by them. They quickly stored all our possessions in the back of a large lorry and soon it was time for them to depart and head for Welling in Kent where John had arranged storage until such time as we had our own home. And so, my time in Germany had come to an end. I was heading to pastures new in England. What would the future bring? No idea, but I could not wait to find out.

Chapter 21

Thursday 15th November 1956. The day finally arrived for us to leave Germany for good and to emigrate and start our new life with John in England. I was so full of hope. I loved John unconditionally. The war years and just after had been torrid. But these last few years with John had been magical. However, the sea journey on this occasion was absolutely awful. The North Sea is not great at the best of times but in winter it can be truly dreadful, and it was. Both me and little Marietta had the most dreadful seasickness. Not a good way to start our trip and a new life in England.

John had travelled up to Harwich to meet us and I was so incredibly happy to see him. I almost fell into his arms. I did not know whether to laugh or cry. I was full of so many emotions, all welling up in me at the same time. Poor little Marietta was still feeling queasy from the sea trip and was not happy at all.

Soon though we were all on the train travelling to Liverpool Street Station and our new life together. At Liverpool Street Station, George again was there to meet us. Poppy and George were so incredibly kind to us. Nothing was ever too much for them. I know, after all, that John was only a relation by marriage, but the way they were with him was like him being a brother. It was so incredibly special.

We travelled on to a place called Belvedere which was only a couple of km from Erith. John had arranged for me and little Marietta to stay for a while in a cheap bed and breakfast. We shared a room to save money. Our room was basic, to say the least, but it was clean and that was the main thing. We had one double bed which we shared.

John was working and staying at The Red Barn, but he had applied for a job as a caretaker with a property management company who were based in Kingston in Surrey. However, the job was in a tenement building just off the Greys Inn Road, in Holborn, Central London. We hoped that this job would come to fruition as it also came with accommodation so the three of us would be together. My bump was getting quite big now and I predicted that I probably only had another six or seven weeks to wait for the new arrival.

Finally, about a week before Christmas, John received notification that his application had been accepted and he had the job. We were all so incredibly happy and grateful. This was the best Christmas present we could have wished for. John would start directly after the New Year.

On Monday 24th December 1956, we travelled back up to London by train to attend an afternoon Children's Carol Service in St Martins in The Field Church, in Trafalgar Square. Marietta still thoroughly enjoyed any trip we could make on a train. It was a wonderful service. Lots of singers and musicians. Although I was not that familiar with most of the carols, one they sang I instantly knew, and that was – Silent Night, or for me it was Stille Nacht.

There were huge crowds all around the fountains in the square despite it being rather cold. It was such a wonderful event, and everyone thoroughly enjoyed themselves and obviously were looking forward to everything that Christmas brings to one and all.

Sadly, all too soon we had to make our way to Charing Cross Station, to catch a train back to Erith. But, we had so much to look forward to, a wonderful Christmas with Poppy and her family, John's new job and most importantly, the birth of our child due in the New Year. Our family of four would be complete and our future looked bright indeed.

Children's Carol Service
Trafalgar Square
Monday, December 24th, 1956

ORGANISED BY THE
DAILY EXPRESS

ST. MARTIN'S JUNIOR CHOIR and the CHOIR OF ST. MARY-OF-THE-ANGELS SONG SCHOOL
CONDUCTED BY JOHN CHURCHILL
Master of Music, St. Martin-in-the-Fields

THE BAND OF THE COLDSTREAM GUARDS
Director of Music : MAJOR D. A. POPE, A.R.C.M.

Christmas Message
by the Vicar of St. Martin-in-the-Fields
The Rev. Austen Williams

I
ONCE IN ROYAL DAVID'S CITY

1.
Once in Royal David's City
Stood a lowly cattle shed,
Where a mother laid her baby,
In a manger for His bed.
Mary was that mother mild,
Jesus Christ her little Child.

2.
He came down to earth from Heaven,
Who is God and Lord of all,
And His shelter was a stable,
And his cradle was a stall ;
With the poor, and mean and lowly,
Lived, on earth, our Saviour holy.

3.
And our eyes at last shall see Him,
Through His own redeeming love,
For that Child, so dear and gentle,
Is our Lord in Heaven above ;
And he leads His children on
To the place where He is gone.

4.
Not in that poor lowly stable,
With the oxen standing by,
We shall see Him ; but in Heaven,
Set at God's right hand on high ;
When like stars His children crowned,
All in white shall wait around.

II
WHILE SHEPHERDS WATCHED

1.
While shepherds watch'd their flocks by
      night,
All seated on the ground,
The angel of the Lord came down,
And glory shone around.

2.
" Fear not," said he ; for mighty dread
Had seized their troubled mind ;
" Glad tidings of great joy I bring
To you and all mankind.

3.
" To you in David's town this day
Is born of David's line
A Saviour, who is Christ the Lord ;
And this shall be the sign :

4.
" The heav'nly Babe you there shall find
To human view displayed,
All meanly wrapp'd in swathing bands,
And in a manger laid."

5.
Thus spake the seraph ; and forthwith
Appear'd a shining throng
Of angels praising God, who thus
Address'd their joyful song :

6.
" All glory be to God on high,
And to the earth be peace ;
Good will henceforth from Heav'n to men
Begin and never cease."

THIS CAROL SHEET IS PRESENTED WITH THE COMPLIMENTS OF THE DAILY EXPRESS

John and little Marietta had great fun feeding the pigeons in Trafalgar Square

So, Christmas came and went and then John moved up to London. Thankfully, the flat/job came with a telephone so at least we were able to talk most days and catch up on news.

Little Marietta and I stayed in the B&B in Belvedere until John moved up to London in the New Year. Then everyone decided that it would be best if I and little Marietta stayed with May and Jack in their house next door to Poppy and George to await the imminent arrival of our baby. He did not want me to have any more worries or deal with yet another move so far along in my pregnancy as that would not be sensible. I needed to rest.

My life has always been full of incidents and this never ever seemed to stop. The next event was on Sunday 20th January 1957. John had come down for the weekend. My time to give birth was imminent and we were playing the waiting game. Poppy had cooked lunch for us all. Everything was going well. Little Marietta was able to have simple conversations with Nell, and Nell absolutely loved this. Little Marietta would sit on the footstall adjacent to Nell's chair, which was located next to the bay window at the front of the lounge, as Nell loved to watch all the movements up and down Collindale Avenue – she didn't like to miss a thing.

I am not entirely sure if they fully understood all of each other's conversations, but it helped little Marietta to learn more.

We had the most wonderful Sunday lunch – a roast chicken dinner and all the trimmings! I had even got used to brussels sprouts, though little Marietta did not care for them at all. Dessert was a bread-and-butter pudding. This was one of John's favourites and Poppy had made it as a special treat for him. After lunch, we all fell into armchairs to relax and chat. Poppy had made me a lovely cup of coffee but she, George and John all had a gin and tonic. I was shattered from doing absolutely nothing.

Typical at this stage of pregnancy, I always seemed to need the loo. I made my way upstairs to the bathroom. Having got in the bathroom/toilet, I locked the door and did my business. When finished, I washed my hands, checked my hair and then tried to unlock the door. To my horror, it was jammed shut and absolutely refused to open. I tried and tried and tried to no avail. I had used this bathroom numerous times and never ever in the past had the lock got stuck.

Finally, I had no choice but to call out and hope someone would hear me. Thankfully they did, and all trouped upstairs to find out what was wrong. With me trying from the inside and them trying from the outside our efforts came to nothing. I was beginning to have visions of giving birth in the bathtub.

John suggested he put his shoulder to the door and bash it in, but Poppy would have none of this. To my utter amazement, she then said she had a solution and she would be with me in a few moments. I had absolutely no idea what on earth she had planned.

The next thing I heard were sounds coming from outside the window. I opened the window to look out to the garden below and saw quite a commotion going on. George was manoeuvring a ladder up against the wall and quickly it was butting up against the bottom of the bathroom windowsill.

Incredibly, as I looked down, I saw Poppy starting her way up the ladder whilst George held it. A couple of minutes later she was at the window and climbing in!

Well my love, she said, we could not have you up here all alone and panicking. Once inside, she went straight to the door, fiddled with the lock and almost instantly, the door was open.

Two days later, I went into labour. I was in the Hainault Nursing Home on Lesney Park Road in Erith.

On 22nd January 1957, at 4 pm, I was delivered another daughter.

Thankfully, all was well and the birth relatively easy. John and I discussed names and we both thought Susannah a nice name. But John said that in England it should be Susan. So, our daughter was named Susan Rosalind Ellen (Ellen being after Poppy & Nell). Both John and I had virtually jet-black hair. Our new daughter was born with no hair whatsoever. The lady in the bed next to me said she thought our daughter would be a redhead. Of course I said this certainly could not be possible as there were no redheads in either family as far as we knew. We would have to wait and see once her hair began to make an appearance. I stayed in the hospital for about a week.

Nowadays, following a birth, you are sent home quite quickly but back then it was at least a week before you were allowed home.

Whilst in the hospital, I received a letter from John. Once again it was full of news. He had managed to buy a few pieces of cheap furniture and hoped that I would be happy with his choices. He had also found a second-hand cot and had painted it white. He was pleased with his work and hoped that I would approve. I was absolutely sure that there was nothing that this man could do that I would not be more than content with.

Chapter 22

At the beginning of February 1957, Marietta, Susan and myself joined John in St Alban's Buildings, Brooke's Court, E.C.1., in the Holborn area of London.

Holborn is practically the centre of London. Charles Dickens, the author, lived in Doughty Street for a while and he put his character 'Pip' from Great Expectations in residence at Barnard's Yard. The area has been associated with the legal profession since medieval times and remains so today. Prudential Insurance Company and the Daily Mirror both had head offices in Holborn at the time. The area is also renowned for diamonds and jewellery with Hatton Garden remaining a focal point for these precious commodities.

This was the start of our family life together. It was an extremely exciting time in many respects though also quite daunting for me and Marietta. But, having dearest John in support, I knew we would manage. John had taken up his position as a caretaker and seemed to enjoy it. Mostly he looked after tenants and their problems and did a little maintenance and security.

The first thing on the agenda to deal with was a school for Marietta. There was an infant/junior church school nearby, St Alban Church of England School and we applied there. Thankfully, she was accepted. Bless her, she was so frightened about going to a new school. What would the children think of a German in their midst? Her English was coming along but she still had much to learn. It must have been so difficult for her. She had been uprooted from her friends and country to somewhere new that only a few years earlier had been at war with her countrymen.

Next was to arrange the christening for Susan. Again, this was reasonably easy to organise as St Alban The Martyr Church was close by so arrangements were made there. By the time of the christening, Susan's hair had started to make an appearance. As predicted by the lady in the bed next to me in the nursing home when Susan was born, it started to come through as ginger. I could not believe it. We were going to have a redhead in the family. I decided quickly that red hair was special and that I would never cut Susan's hair – I wanted her to eventually have long red hair that I could plait into ponytails or leave long flowing down the length of her back.

Susan was baptised on 2nd June 1957 – which also happened to be our 1st wedding anniversary. It was a lovely day. Poppy and George came and, of course, were God Parents, which they both were so happy about. We knew that, without a doubt they would be perfect as they would always love and cherish Susan as their own. Many years later, on 15th November 1970, Susan was confirmed, and her baptism details were added to the confirmation information. From looking at the writing on the confirmation certificate, I am almost certain that this had been filled out by Susan as it definitely looks like a child writing. I had forgotten about this until I came across it again whilst searching for documents to accompany my ramblings.

DIOCESE OF SOUTHWARK

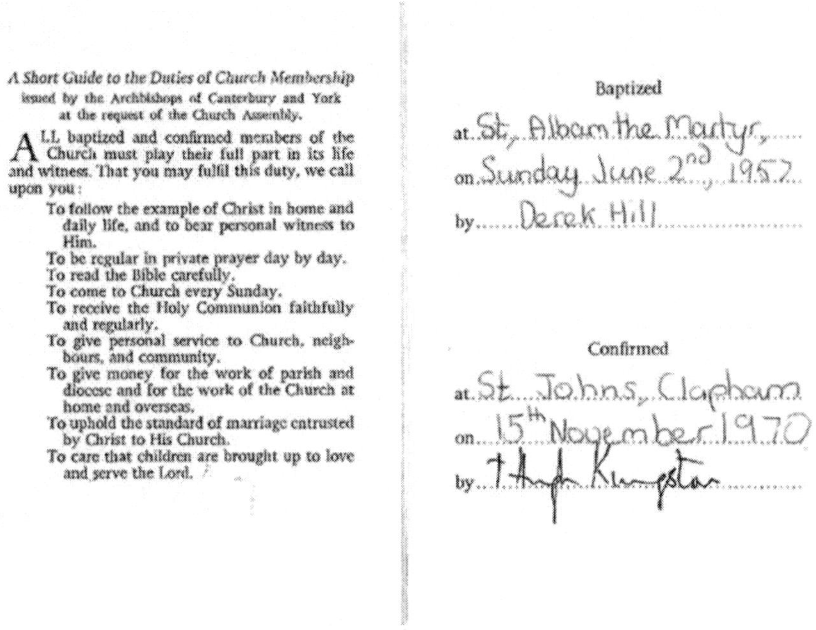

Baptized

at St, Alban the Martyr,
on Sunday June 2nd, 1952.
by Derek Hill

Confirmed

at St. Johns, Clapham
on 15th November 1970
by T Hugh Kingston

Susan's baptism and confirmation certificate

Susan was growing up quickly. We were so lucky as she was not a difficult child at all. She slept well and rarely cried. John was so delighted with his daughter. Of course, John stilled popped out for a regular pint at the local pub. Whilst there, he became friends with a photographer that worked for a national newspaper, The Daily Mirror. Jim was such a nice man. He would often pop round to see us armed with his camera. He took so many photos of us all from when Susan was first born and for several years after. They are all large black and white photos around 7 x 5 inches, though a couple are more like an A4 size. I have included a few of them in the book that are among my favourites.

Erika, Susan and John – 1957

Marietta was managing at school. It was not easy for her at all, but her English was coming along much better. As soon as I had arrived in England, I chose to stop speaking German. John could not understand German, and also Marietta had to quickly learn English, and this was the best way. I also chose not to speak any German to Susan. Apart from John not speaking German, the main reason was that I wanted a complete and absolute break from Germany. No German would be spoken and nothing to do with the war would be watched on TV or at the pictures. I wanted to forget that I was German. I had far too many horrible memories from the war years and just after. The atrocities I witnessed were often in my mind, and speaking German seemed to bring it back all too clearly. Therefore, not speaking German was for me the best way forward.

Our lives continued from day to day much the same and little change. Then, out of the blue in June 1958, John's employers asked him to transfer to an alternative development. This one was south of the River Thames between Vauxhall and Stockwell. So, again, we had an upheaval. But our belongings were minimal, and it did not take long to pack and be off to a new home.

Chapter 23

Our new home was flat 38, Atholl Mansions, South Lambeth Road, SW8. The buildings were built c. 1895 and were basic. They were located on both sides of South Lambeth Road and were named Atholl Mansions and Albert Mansions on the left, and Victoria Mansions and Victoria House on the right. They consisted of six floors, including the ground floor, and approximately 100 flats. We had the caretaker's flat on the ground floor of Atholl Mansions.

South Lambeth Road. Atholl and Albert Mansions on left and Victoria Mansions and
House on right
Source: Lambeth Archive

Atholl Mansions and Radnor Terrace
Source: Lambeth Archive

In the photo above, the caretaker's flat is the one at the bottom of the block, adjacent to the houses on Radnor Terrace to the right.

It should have had two bedrooms, but one was used as the caretaker's office. The reason being is that as well as acting as security and managing simple maintenance, John was also responsible for collecting rents. In those days, most people rented and would pay their rent, in cash, on a weekly basis. They had a rent book which they would bring to the office and John would update it to show that they had paid. It is strange what you remember. Amazingly, I can still remember the number of the telephone in the office. It was Macauley 5411. In those days, we were in the Nine Elms area exchange with the designation of Macauley. Later this became 622 – 01 622 5411.

With only one bedroom, this meant that Marietta had to sleep on a put-you-up folding bed in the office. Of course, this was not ideal in the least and I know how unhappy this made her. But there was nowhere else. From the front door, there was a long straight corridor. On the right side the first room was a small kitchen, then a sitting room, then the bedroom. On the left side was a small

147

bathroom. At the end of the corridor was the office. From the office, there was an external door that opened directly on to South Lambeth Road. This was the door that tenants or visitors used when coming into the office.

There was not the luxury of central heating. All we had was an electric heater in the sitting room – that was it. In the winter we would have ice on the inside the windows when it was cold. So, layers of clothing and jumpers were the norm. My knitting again came in handy as we all needed warm clothing for the winter months.

Marietta had now reached the age where she had to go to senior school. The nearest was Vauxhall Manor but unfortunately, they did not have room for her. So, instead, she had to go to Priory Grove School in Stockwell and that was quite a walk for her every day, regardless of the weather. I think kids were much tougher in those days. Today they are mollycoddled and driven everywhere. Marietta would moan, of course, but it fell on deaf ears.

John was particularly happy with the location of our new home as it was literally only a few steps to the nearest pub which was The Wheatsheaf. He found it hard to go for more than a day without a pint of his beloved beer. I sometimes wondered if he cared more for his beer than he did of me. It was like he would have withdrawal symptoms if for some reason he could not have his daily pint. So, he would, most evenings, pop up the road for his daily dose. He was also a smoker which I have mentioned before. He did not smoke all day long, by no means, but he did like a cigarette. Especially when down the pub!

The Wheatsheaf Pub – South Lambeth Road
Date of photo: 1967
Picture source: Timothy Keane

Whilst in the army, John played darts and snooker competitively and was, on a number of occasions, the army darts champion. He had several lovely trophies which he proudly cleaned and polished. They were all sat on a sideboard in our front room. I always kept them on display. However, during a move in the 1980s, they had been all packed up into a box. It was months later when I thought about them and searched for them and sadly, I could not find them. I was heartbroken. I could only assume that the removal men had stolen them. I had no proof and there was little I could do.

They were not worth any monetary value, only sentimental value. The only proof of their existence is a photo of Susan with them all.

Susan with John's trophies he received/won whilst in the army

The other thing related to beer that John collected, which I still have, are miniature Whitbread Inn signs. They are metallic/aluminium and in order to collect them you had to visit the pub, have a pint and you would get one. So, work out how many pubs John visited to get the whole of the first series! They are the size of a playing card. On the front is the pub sign and name. On the reverse are brief details about the pub and the number of the card and the series. I believe there were three series in all, but John only collected from the first one – 50 cards in all. The collection would have been predominately acquired during the 1950s.

Whitbread Inn pub signs – complete first series from the 1950s

Chapter 24

We were lucky in relation to shops as we had many close to us. Just past Atholl Mansions heading towards Stockwell, was a road to the right called Wilcox Road. Halfway down was a fantastic market where everything we needed on a daily basis could be purchased. The area was always a hive of activity and invariably busy. It was the main shopping district in the area, so everyone shopped there. Bargains could be had if you knew where to look and were willing to negotiate.

It was generally quite noisy and often there was rubbish strewn all over the place. There were many fruit and vegetable stalls. The stallholders would shout out their prices and offers to encourage you to buy only from them. It was like a competition between them of who could shout the loudest. Each trying to out-do the other and make you stop at their stall. Most of the time though I doubt if anyone knew what they were shouting about as it was never particularly clear.

Wilcox Road Market – in the background, you can see the chimney pots of Atholl and
Albert Mansions
Source: Lambeth Archive

These were the days when you would shop in individual shops for your daily goods going down one side of the market and then coming back the other way. Armed of course with a trolley to deposit all your purchases in.

Kaye's Bakery on the corner with Hartington Road sold the most wonderful bread and cakes. On Good Friday, it was the only shop open in the area and simply to sell hot cross buns straight out of the oven. They were so scrumptious especially with lots of butter.

Brunning's the butchers on the left going towards Wandsworth Road always had good quality meat. There were always copious amounts of sawdust on the floor.

Charlie Panetta's café was on the right-hand side walking towards Wandsworth Road. At the front of the shop was a window with a sliding panel. You could take a bowl from home and they would fill it up with ice cream – all for a few pennies. A real treat. Of course, you had to get home quickly or it would melt!

Just along from Charlie's was the launderette – obviously, a frequent visitor here. No luxury of having a washing machine in our flat so weekly visits to the launderette was the norm. All the dirty washing would be put into a trolley and wheeled to the launderette for washing and drying. Sometimes if I were busy, Marietta would take it for me on a Saturday morning.

Pete's fish and chip shop was a regular haunt. If having a take-away, the fish would be wrapped up in newspaper. Two bob fish and a six of chips 2/6d.

Mannie Harris was a wool shop. Often, I would purchase skeins of wool from here as I still had my passion for knitting. Something was always on the go.

Ivy's was a sweet shop. I think this was one of Marietta's favourite places. She would love to have a jamboree bag for 6d which contained all sorts of different sweeties: gobstoppers, blackjacks, flying saucers, parma violets, fruit gums, coconut mushrooms, etc.

Plus, Pothecary's the greengrocers, Peter the family outfitters, Ernie Noad Shoe Shop and lots of others.

So, as I have said, everything we could want was basically available to buy on our doorstep.

Wilcox Road market looking messy
Source: Lambeth Archive

Wilcox Road approaching South Lambeth Road
Source: Lambeth Archive

With the abundance of fresh fruit available from the market, I was able to make one of my cook's specialities that everyone absolutely loved. This was fresh fruit flans. Generally, the flans were with seasonal fruit or with a lemon curd. Though on occasion I did use tinned pineapple rings and stick a maraschino cocktail cherry into the centre hole.

I had two tin tins which had crimped edges that I brought with me from Germany. One was around 12 inches across and the other half the size.

The base was shortcrust which would be baked and then left to cool. I would then decorate the whole flan case with fresh strawberries. Next, and most importantly, was the glaze that went over the top of it all. I had tried a number of glazes that I could purchase locally but they simply did not work as well. The only ones that were perfect were Dr Oetker clear cake glaze. When I left Germany, I brought a few packs with me, but they were long gone. So, I had to rely on my dear friend Inge in Berlin. Once a year she would put a dozen or so into an envelope and send them to me.

My fruit flans have always been popular with everyone. It has been a tradition for me to bake one and take with me when visiting friends or family. Woe betide if I did not turn up with one, I could risk being turned away at the door. They were quite delicate to transport so much care had to be ensured. I had a large flattish plastic round box that they fitted into. This then went into a flat round carrier bag with long handles that I had made myself specifically for this purpose.

Our lives continued and, gradually, Marietta and I were becoming used to the area and the people. Overall, most of those that we encountered were polite. But if I was without John, on occasion, I was the victim of racism. Everything was fine until I opened my mouth. As soon as they realised that I was German, barriers would often come up. It was still quite soon after the war and memories were long.

I was spat at, was asked to get off a bus on one occasion and quite often refused to be served in certain shops. This was incredibly distressing, and I chose not to share it with John. He would have been mortified and challenged those concerned. So, I simply did not shop anywhere where I knew I was not wanted. Sadly, racism is still rife. I do not think humanity will ever learn that to be kind to one another is extremely rewarding.

As well as shopping on Wilcox Road, we often would get a No.2 Route Master bus to the nearby area of Brixton. All buses had a driver and a conductor. The conductor had a machine around his/her neck for dispensing tickets. Being that South Lambeth Road was a main road, we were fortunate to have a number of buses going by. Some going to Brixton then on towards Tulse Hill, Crystal Palace, Norwood and Streatham. Others heading south towards Clapham, Balham, Tooting and Merton.

Route Master bus number 2

Route Master bus number 2 together with a bus ticket cost 4d (old currency)

Brixton is a district of South London, within the London Borough of Lambeth. It is mainly residential with a prominent street market and substantial retail sector. It is a multi-ethnic community, with a large percentage of its population of Afro-Caribbean descent.

In 1948, the first wave of immigrants (492 individuals) who formed the British African-Caribbean community, arrived in 1948, at Tilbury Docks on the HMT Empire Windrush from Jamaica, and were temporarily housed in the Clapham South deep shelter. The nearest labour exchange (jobcentre) was on Coldharbour Lane, Brixton, and the new arrivals spread out into local accommodation. Many immigrants only intended to stay in Britain for a few years but, although a number returned to the Caribbean, the majority remained to settle permanently.

The arrival of the passengers has become an important landmark in the history of modern Britain, and the image of West Indians filing off its gangplank has come to symbolise the beginning of modern British multicultural society.

HMT Empire Windrush

The market in Brixton was absolutely brilliant. Much bigger than Wilcox Road. It was a vibrant community. There were many different kinds of shops, often selling food items that I had never heard of. Many were imported for the local Caribbean community. I suppose it was a way of helping them to adapt being so far away from home. It must have been difficult for them and I could definitely relate to that.

It was in a delicatessen in Brixton Arcade that I was able to buy supplies for my addiction! Do not panic, it was not something sinister but simply my absolute love of freshly brewed coffee. This had been a passion from when I was a teenager. I definitely could not abide the taste of tea. Coffee was my hot drink of choice. I would buy a small quantity of beans each week. Buying beans was slightly cheaper than buying ground coffee. When I got home, I would use a grinder that I had brought with me from Germany, to grind the beans. It was a manual one. There was a small opening on the top where the beans went. Then simply turn the handle and grounds would appear in the drawer at the bottom. Once done, the grounds would then be put into a sealed jar for later use.

A vintage coffee grinder

To go with the coffee, another little treat was the cream from the top of the milk bottle. The cream could be clearly seen through the transparent glass at the top of the bottle as it was a deeper colour. Following homogenisation some years later, this indulgence disappeared.

Milk was delivered each morning by a United Dairies milkman using his electric motor float and the cream at the top of each bottle was mine! Heaven forbids anyone taking this for themselves.

Birds were cheeky though. They also knew about the wonderful treat at the top of a milk bottle. We lived in a flat, so our milk was protected. But when I walked along Rosetta Street, which was at the back of Atholl Mansions, on my way to the Wilcox Road market, I often noticed that milk sat on doorsteps had little piercings in the foil top – birds were the culprits.

My other favourite shop in Brixton was a John Lewis store called Bon Marche. This was absolutely brilliant for fabrics, dress or jumper patterns and skeins of wool. Plus, all the other accessories that I might need. My passion and love for dressmaking never ceased and I absolutely loved to be working on something whether it was dresses for the girls, soft furnishing for our home or even suits for John. I was always making something whether dressmaking or knitting, something was always on the go. I never bought any cardigans, jumpers, dresses, coats, or soft furnishings for John, myself, the girls or our home unless I had no choice. It was cheaper to make them myself.

Bon Marche had a little tearoom on the top floor. As a special treat, we would all drop in and have our drink plus a large slice of cake or maybe a toasted teacake or a bun.

One other memory from this store was the system to pay. Each sales floor had a pneumatic tube system which was used to transport sales slips and money, in a small canister with a screw top, from the salesperson to a centralised cash room, where cashiers could make change, reference credit records and so on, and then the change and receipt would whisk its way back to the sales floor. All seems rather convoluted but actually it worked well. It always fascinated me watching the canister whiz off up the tube and then waiting patiently for the receipt and change to appear a few minutes later.

One for the first things I acquired, when we settled into Atholl Mansions, was a Singer treadle sewing machine. We could not afford to buy a new sewing machine, so I hunted around, spoke to neighbours and asked them to look out for one for me. I also spoke to the rag and bone man in case he came across one on his travels. Thankfully, it was not long before one was found for me.

This was from a lady on Tradescant Road, which ran at the back of Victoria Mansions across South Lambeth Road from us. She was moving and no longer had the need for the machine. She only wanted a few pounds for it so it was a bargain. It proved to be old but in particularly good condition so of course, as soon as I saw it, I knew I had to have it.

John paid for it, borrowed a sack barrow and wheeled it home!

I cannot imagine how many things I made from this cheap old Singer treadle machine. It was always on the go for many, many years. John took a while to get used to the clanking noises it made as I treadled away for hours. It did rather rattle a lot.

Bon Marche played a huge part in this. I would go there and buy remnants of materials and then make up the patterns. McCall's or Simplicity were favourites. Being frugal, I would make every variation of the one pattern: short sleeves, long sleeves, no sleeves, etc. The girls were used to having the same pattern dresses but with different sleeves.

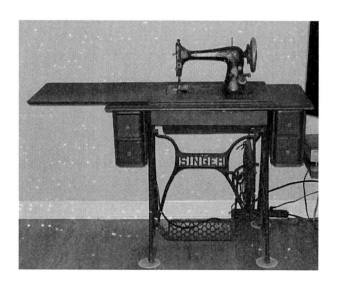

Singer treadle sewing machine

Simplicity pattern from 1960s

Susan was growing up so quickly. Often John would take her out in her pram when he had places/people to visit. Actually, it was pretty rare in those days to see a man on his own wheeling a pushchair. Also, as John wasn't a young man, I did wonder at times if people assumed he was her grandfather rather than her father. If he had to go to his employers in Kingston, he would sometimes take Susan with him. She loved this as it meant getting on a train.

Kingston Upon Thames (spelled with hyphens until 1965 and sometimes abbreviated to Kingston), is a town, former manor, ecclesiastical parish and borough now within Greater London, England, formerly within the county of Surrey. It is situated on the River Thames, about 10 m above sea level and 16 km southwest of Charing Cross (deemed the geographical centre of London). It is notable as the ancient market town in which Saxon kings were crowned and today is the administrative centre of the Royal Borough of Kingston upon Thames.

The large historic parish of Kingston became absorbed in modern times into the Municipal Borough of Kingston upon Thames, reformed in 1835 and from 1893 has been the location of Surrey County Hall, extraterritorially in terms of local government administration. Since 1965 Kingston has been a part of Greater London.

This gave me a break to get on with things at home. Although we had Vauxhall and Kennington Parks within walking distance from us, which were lovely to picnic in or stroll around, the country was still relatively new to me and I liked to go out and about, further afield, if I could to see more of our surrounding areas. Hence, now and again we would venture out by bus or train to see other parts of London.

It was only a short walk to Vauxhall Station and from there on one occasion we took a train and visited The Royal Botanical Gardens at Kew. This is the most wonderful place to while away a few hours, especially if the weather is nice.

Kew Gardens is a botanic garden in Southwest London that houses the largest and most diverse botanical and mycological collections in the world. Founded in 1840, from the exotic garden at Kew Park in Middlesex, England, its living collections includes some of the 27,000 taxa curated by Royal Botanic Gardens, Kew, while the herbarium, which is one of the largest in the world, has over 8.5 million preserved plant and fungal specimens. The library contains more than 750,000 volumes, and the illustrations collection contains more than 175,000 prints and drawings of plants. It is one of London's top tourist attractions and is a World Heritage Site.

Marietta and Susan in Kew Gardens May 1959

Chapter 25

Our lives seemed to be happy and content. John was enjoying his job and that was important to us. It must have been so difficult for him, in many ways, as he had been in the army for such a long time. His whole life, though, was still managed on a strict routine, and the drumming into him throughout his military career of method and procedure was always paramount to him.

Marietta was managing at school. It was not easy for her though, but she made a few friends. One was Eileen and she often would pop in to see Marietta and us. She was a lovely girl and I have many fond memories of her. Our day-to-day routine was much the same each and every day. John was always up early and ready in his office for any callers. Marietta went to school and I busied myself looking after Susan, and I was still knitting and dressmaking. We lived very frugally and did not waste a penny. Any extra shillings were saved for a rainy day.

As mentioned, ages ago, John had two sons from his marriage to Alice: Gary and Michael. They were both grown up now. Gary was married and came to visit in South Lambeth Road with his wife Barbara and baby daughter Sandra.

John, me, Marietta, Gary, Barbara with Sandra and Susan, all took a walk along the Albert Embankment alongside the River Thames.

Gary and Barbara went on to have another daughter, who they named Karen. Sadly, their marriage was not to last and they divorced.

Barbara, Gary and baby Sandra with John, Marietta and Susan – Millbank 1958

Gary and John – Millbank 1958

Gary also served his country for a number of years as his father did, but in the Royal Navy rather than the army. John's other son, Michael, married Carol in 1961, and they were to have two children: Michaela was born in 1965, and Darren was born 1967.

In May 1960, I took Marietta and Susan for a short break in Torquay. John was unable to come with us due to commitments at home. We stayed at the Lansdowne Hotel on Babbacombe Road.

Torquay is a seaside town in Devon, England, part of the unitary authority area of Torbay. It lies 29 km south of the county town of Exeter and 45 km east-northeast of Plymouth, on the north of Tor Bay, adjoining the neighbouring town of Paignton on the west of the bay and across from the fishing port of Brixham. The town's economy, like Brixham's, was initially based upon fishing and agriculture, but in the early 19th century it began to develop into a fashionable seaside resort, initially frequented by members of the Royal Navy during the Napoleonic Wars while the Royal Navy anchored in the bay.

Later, as the town's fame spread, it was popular with Victorian society. Renowned for its mild climate (for the UK), the town earned the nickname the English Riviera. The writer Agatha Christie was born in the town and lived there during her early years.

To my delight, John sent me a couple of letters whilst we were away. To receive them reminded me of the many that he had sent previously. They were, as usual, full of day-to-day news. He hoped we were having a good time and could not wait until his family was home again as he was missing us so very much. It was a shame that he could not travel with us, but I knew he would be waiting for us, arms open wide, at Vauxhall Station when we arrived back home.

Marietta and Susan in Torquay May 1960

As you can see from the above, I did like to dress the girls the same. Marietta did not like this at all. She was sneaky and would try to make sure that any dress which was the same as Susan's was dirty, so she did not have to wear the same as Susan.

The next event was in September 1962, and Susan starting infants' school. This was Wyvil Primary School and was only a few minutes' walk from our flat in the direction of Vauxhall. It was a Victorian building having been built in 1876. Susan quickly settled in and made lots of friends.

Since living in Atholl Mansions, it had become a tradition each 5th November (Guy Fawkes – bonfire night) that John arranged a treat for the children living in the flats and on Rosetta Street. He would save a few shillings throughout the year and on 5th November in the large yard at the back of the flats, he would fill an old oil drum with wood to make a fire. All the children from the flats and Rosetta Street would gather around and each of them would have at least a sparkler. They would sing songs, play games and have a laugh. No one in the area had much money so this was a treat for everyone. Sometimes, John would have enough money for a few rockets, and they were a special addition.

Chapter 26

Towards the end of 1962, we began to worry as the weather forecast going forward was awful and the Nation was heading towards the coldest and longest spell of winter on record. None of us though appreciated actually how appalling it was going to be. Our flat had little heating, only a small electric fire in the front room. We knew we were going to have a sorry time, and probably did not appreciated how absolutely horrible it was going to be.

At the beginning of December, it was foggy, and London suffered its last great smog before clean air legislation and the reduction in the use of coal fires had their full effect. A wintry outbreak brought snow to the country on 12–13 December. A cold easterly set in on 22 December as an anticyclone formed over Scandinavia, drawing cold continental winds from Russia. Throughout the Christmas period, the Scandinavian high collapsed, but a new one formed near Iceland, bringing northerly winds.

Poppy and George had invited us to spend Christmas with them. We would not be able to stay in their house as not enough room but, once again, May and Jack next door had offered for us to use their spare bedroom to sleep in.

We wanted to go, but getting there and back was not going to be an easy task because the weather forecast was awful. But we decided to give it a go. In the past, George had driven up to collect us, but we thought this journey too perilous for him. Therefore, we would get the number 88 bus from South Lambeth Road to Trafalgar Square, walk around to Charing Cross Station and get a train.

We set off looking like we were going on an artic expedition. All dressed in thick winter clothing, hats, gloves and boots. We packed only the bare minimum into a small suitcase that John carried. Marietta had a rucksack into which we put the Christmas presents we had bought. I could not bear to wear a rucksack, so I had a large holdall that I carried with one hand whilst keeping hold of Susan in the other.

Our journey began on Saturday 22nd December with the intention of travelling back on Boxing Day as John was to be at work again on Thursday 27th. We knew that buses and trains were in action but that timetables were not being always being adhered to. It was basically going to be potluck, but it was definitely worthwhile having a go. The girls though it all a great adventure which they were thoroughly looking forward to.

The nearest bus stop was close by, outside the Wheatsheaf Pub. We must have looked a funny sight to anyone seeing us.

Thankfully, it was not long before the bus arrived, and we all trundled on. The usual twenty-minute journey took forty-five minutes, but we finally arrived at Trafalgar Square. Seeing London bedecked in a blanket of snow was quite incredible and, if the forecast came true, there would be more snow to come and more than anyone had seen before.

Slowly we made our way to the station being careful not to slip on the icy surfaces.

Once inside the station we relaxed a bit and then kept our fingers crossed that there would be a train reasonable soon. Thankfully, at the ticket office they said that we would have to wait maybe an hour and then there would be a train to Dartford and this would be stopping at Erith.

John used a public telephone box to call Poppy and give her a rough estimate of when we would arrive. George intended to pick us up at Erith Station which was wonderful as there were no buses from the station to near Collindale Avenue and it was doubtful that a taxi could be found. Walking was not an option. It was too far, and mostly uphill, so there was no way that we could manage this.

Armed with our tickets we made our way to near the platform where the train was expected. As Charing Cross is a terminus, we would see the train arrive and once all passengers were off, we expected we would be able to get on and then simply wait for the train to leave.

As we sat playing I-Spy, Susan spotted a vending machine. She had a great passion for chocolate. This was a Cadbury milk chocolate machine and the cost I believe was 6d. Of course, John always spoilt the girls and bought them a bar each.

I had made a flask of coffee for the journey and John and I enjoyed this together with a piece of fruitcake.

Finally, the train arrived, and we were soon on our way. Travelling down to Erith looking out of the carriage window, it certainly gave us an insight as to the extent of the awful weather. We knew from watching the news and reading newspapers that it was horrendous but worse was to come and we hoped it would not arrive until we were back home again.

Eventually, we arrived at Erith Station and alighted the train.

George was outside in the car waiting for us.

He said he would take us a long way round to their house because trying to get up the hill on the Bexley Road towards Northumberland Heath was not an easy task. He had come that way to the station and it was treacherous. It was not much further to drive, and we soon arrived at the house all safe and sound.

Poppy was at the door to greet us and we all rushed in to get in front of the open coal fire to warm ourselves.

The few days we spent with them all were wonderful. They were always such magnificent hosts. Poppy was an excellent cook and we had the most exceptional Christmas day.

They had a large circle of friends. The lounge/diner was around 25ft I suppose and all around both rooms was a picture rail about 1 foot below ceiling level. Christmas cards were sat on the rail, about six inches apart, all around the whole room. I was astonished to see so many cards. There must have been getting on for a hundred of them.

Christmas Day morning was always open house and you could expect from two and to thirty or more friends to turn up for a drink. Generally, people just popped in, had a drink, stayed for a while and then left again. It was such a lovely environment.

All too soon our time to go home again arrived and we were on the return journey. Thankfully, we arrived back home in Atholl Mansions just before the onslaught of absolutely atrocious weather. Far worse than any of us could have imagined.

Significant snowfall occurred as the air mass moved south, and parts of Southern England had heavy snow late on 26–27 December. The cold air became firmly established. On 29 and 30 December 1962, a blizzard swept across South West England and Wales. Snow drifted to more than 20 feet deep in places, driven by gale-force easterly winds, blocking roads and railways. The snow stranded villagers and brought down power lines.

The near-freezing temperatures meant that the snow cover lasted for more than two months in some areas.

Snow was 6 inches deep in Manchester city centre, 9 inches in Wythenshawe and about 18 inches at Keele University in Staffordshire. By the end of the month, there were snowdrifts 8 feet deep in Kent and 15 feet deep in the west. With an average temperature of –2.1°C (28.2°F), January 1963 remains the coldest month since January 1814 in Central England, although in Northern England, Scotland and Northern Ireland February 1947 was colder and December 2010 was colder in Northern Ireland. Much of England and Wales was covered in snow throughout the month.

The country experienced temperatures as low as −19.4°C (−2.9°F) at Achany in Sutherland on the 11th. Freezing fog was a hazard for most of the country. In January 1963, the sea froze for a mile from shore at Herne Bay, Kent. The sea froze inshore in many places, removing many British inland waters birds' usual last resort of finding food in estuaries and shallow sea. The sea froze 4 miles out to sea from Dunkirk. The upper reaches of the River Thames froze over, although it did not freeze in Central London, partly due to the hot effluent from two thermal power stations: Battersea and Bankside.

The removal of the multi-arched London Bridge, which had obstructed the river's free flow, and the addition of the river embankments kept the river from freezing in London as it had in earlier times.

On 20 January 1963, 283 workers had to be rescued by RAF helicopters from Fylingdales, where they had been snowbound for several days.

The ice was thick enough in some places that people were skating on it, and on 22 January, a car was driven across the frozen Thames at Oxford. Icicles hung from many roof gutters, some as long as 3 feet. On 25 January, there was a brief thaw that lasted three days. Snow continued to fall in February 1963, which was stormy with winds reaching Force 8 on the Beaufort scale (gale-force winds).

A 36-hour blizzard caused heavy drifting snow in most parts of the country. Drifts reached 20 feet in some areas and gale-force winds reached up to 81 mph. On the Isle of Man, wind speeds were recorded at 119 mph.

The 6 March was the first morning of the year without frost in Britain. Temperatures rose to 17°C (62.6°F) and the remaining snow disappeared.

No.2 bus struggling in the snow and ice

Without a doubt, this winter was the toughest I could ever remember. It was unbelievably cold. Many services came to a stop and day-to-day food items were often hard to find. But we managed. John was incredibly busy during this period. Pipes were frozen in many of the buildings and a number of tenants were vulnerable. We did what we could to help but it was often just as difficult for us. Everyone rallied around though and helped where they could.

Marietta had a dreadful time getting to and from school. Obviously, we felt that she should at least try and get there. It was not easy for her at all. On a few occasions, she got there only to find the school closed as the heating had failed. So, she had a wasted journey and had to come home again.

For Susan, getting to school was not so much of a problem as it was close by. But even so, the snow was piled up everywhere and, as with Marietta, sometimes we would get there only to be turned away as the school was not open. Once March 1963 arrived and the thaw began, we all breathed a sigh of relief.

None of us would ever want to go through the same conditions again. All in all, this was a horrible time for everyone.

Chapter 27

There were a number of unusual traditions in London that I was not used to in Germany. One I mentioned earlier, was the rag and bone man. These men would travel around the area with a horse and cart collecting unwanted rags, metal, clothing, furniture and other waste items which they would basically recycle and sell on to merchants. You knew they were in the area by the ringing of a handbell and a call, though I could never understand what they were saying. But it was not just me with the problem, most neighbours would also say that they had no idea what was being shouted.

Another tradition was the toffee apple seller. He would come around weekly on a bicycle that had a large wicker hamper on the front. You could buy a toffee apple and, for an extra penny, he would dip it in desiccated coconut. I could not imagine that he made much of a living from this. But he was around the whole time we lived on South Lambeth Road.

We would regularly hear from Poppy and George and saw them as often as we could. They did, on occasion, come to visit us but space was difficult, so it was preferable to visit them in Erith. I was so fond of Poppy and George. Having them in our lives was important to me. They were the only 'relations' that John had. I had no relations left in Germany, as far as I was aware, so this family meant such a great deal to me. Susan was growing up quickly and celebrated her 6th birthday in January 1963, and Marietta celebrated her 16th birthday in June.

In June 1963, John and I had the most terrible scare. One Saturday morning, Susan was outside playing in the yard with a bunch of local children. It was safe in those days and she would often go out in the morning and play with her friends for a couple of hours. Of course, we would always pop out and check on her. This I did and to my horror, none of the children were around. I searched and searched to no avail. I went in and got John. We both again looked everywhere and nothing.

John then spoke to a neighbour, Mrs Wilkins, and asked if she had seen them. She told us that she had heard the children speaking about going to the park. This would be Vauxhall Park – a ten-minute walk and on the opposite side of the busy South Lambeth Road.

Vauxhall Park is a Green Flag Award-winning municipal park in Vauxhall, South London, run by Lambeth Council. It occupies an 8.5-acre site and was created at a cost of around £45,000 and opened in 1890 by Prince Albert. The land was purchased from a local developer under the Vauxhall Park Act 1888.

Henry Fawcett's garden forms part of the park. A statue of Fawcett was erected in the park in 1897 but has since been replaced by a plaque. The park is famous for its lavender garden and annual lavender harvest.

I was in a terrible state. John set off to the park to check there and I waited at home in case she had gone somewhere else.

The one place in the park that the children loved was the play area that had a sandpit, swings, slide, roundabout and see-saw. Susan loved going here so I could understand if her friends said they were going that she would want to go too.

When John got there, he spied her immediately. Her red hair was instantly recognisable. He grabbed her and smacked her bottom. He then dragged her out of the park. They crossed the lights at Fentiman Road, and outside Brand's Factory, she received another smack. When he got home with her, she received another smack from me. I think this was the only time John and I had smacked her. I suppose it was out of worry more than anything. Suffice to say she never did anything like this ever again.

Susan (second from left) and friends having fun in the yard at back of Atholl Mansions

Another story concerning Susan was a trip we made in July 1963 to Clapham Common. The Common was only a short bus ride on a number 88 along South Lambeth Road towards Stockwell, over the roundabout and then onwards to Clapham.

Clapham Common is a large triangular urban park in Clapham, South London. Originally common land for the parishes of Battersea and Clapham, it was converted to parkland under the terms of the Metropolitan Commons Act 1878. It is 220 acres (89 hectares) of green space, with three ponds and a Victorian bandstand. It is overlooked by large Georgian and Victorian mansions and nearby Clapham Old Town.

Holy Trinity Clapham, an 18th-century Georgian church overlooking the park, is important in the history of the evangelical Clapham Sect. Half of the park is within the London Borough of Wandsworth and the other half is within the London Borough of Lambeth.

Originally common land for the parishes of Battersea and Clapham, William Hewer was among the early Londoners to build adjacent to it. Samuel Pepys, the diarist, died at Hewer's house in 1703. The land had been used for cricket in 1700 and was drained in the 1760s, and from the 1790s onwards, fine houses

178

were built around the common as fashionable dwellings for wealthy business people in what was then a village detached from Metropolitan London.

Some later residents were members of the Clapham Sect of evangelical reformers, including Lord Teignmouth and Henry Thornton, the banker and abolitionist. In 1911, Scottish evangelist and teacher Oswald Chambers (1874–1917) founded and was principal of the Bible Training College in Clapham Common, an 'embarrassingly elegant' property situated at 45 North Side that had been purchased by the Pentecostal League of Prayer. Excerpts of Chambers weekly addresses to the student body at the college were published in 1934, by his wife Gertrude (Biddy) Hobbs in the book *My Utmost for His Highest*, perhaps one of the most widely read Christian devotional books (39 languages, 13 million copies).

J. M. W. Turner painted 'View on Clapham Common' between 1800 and 1805, showing that even though the common had been drained, it still remained 'quite a wild place'.

The common was converted to parkland under the terms of the Metropolitan Commons Act in 1878. As London expanded in the 19th century, Clapham was absorbed into the capital, with most of the remaining palatial or agricultural estates replaced with terraced housing by the early 1900s. During World War II, storage bunkers were built on the Battersea Rise side of the common; two mounds remain.

Often in the summer a large county show/agricultural fair would be held here. There was of course a huge fun fair with lots of fantastic rides. Plus, many other great events such as show jumping, falconry, military displays and food exhibitions. There were competitions, with prizes awarded by judges, allowing farmers and breeders to show off their cattle or crops. Together with an abundance of craft and food stalls, as well as activities, for locals and visitors to enjoy.

Young's Brewery, who at the time were based in Wandsworth, would bring several of their shire horses to the event.

They were a sight to behold being such enormous horses. Children were given the opportunity to sit on top of one. We thought Susan would like this. John picked her up and placed her on top of one of the horses. Almost instantaneously she screamed the house down and wanted off. She did not want to stay anywhere near the horses, so we immediately grabbed her and quickly move away from the area. Straight away she calmed down.

Having reassured her we would not venture near them again it transpired that it was not the size of the horses that freaked her out but their hairy hoofs. She has never particularly liked horses ever since and tends to avoid them.

Marietta left school in the summer of 1963 and got a job in a factory called Freemans located at 139 Clapham Road between Kennington and Stockwell. It was around a 20-minute walk for her along Dorset Road, which was at the back of Victoria Mansions opposite us, so not too bad.

Freemans was founded in 1905, selling initially only clothing through a catalogue distributed around the UK. In 1937, they expanded their product lines to include household goods such as vacuum cleaners and washing machines. Being that their large premises were so close to Central London, the building was bombed during WW2 and sadly, 23 members of staff were killed. However, the company continued to trade. By 1950, the post-war boom meant people were left with more money than they knew what to do with.

Freemans capitalised on this and extended its catalogue even more, becoming highly successful. In 1963, Freemans PLC was floated on the stock market as it became a public limited company and installed its first computer, being the first mail-order company to do so. This was just one example of how Freemans built a name as the most pioneering mail-order company in the UK, followed by the introduction of telephone ordering and digital catalogues.

Marietta in 1962

In August 1963, we all went on a holiday to Kent. John wanted to show us around where he grew up. It was so nice that we could all go together. We visited Folkestone and the surrounding areas.

We stayed at a small bed and breakfast hotel called Cliffe Lodge which was near the sea front.

Even after all the time we had known each other, John was still reticent to talk about his family. I, of course, respected his wishes and never pushed him on the subject as I knew only too well that he had no wish whatsoever to talk about them.

However, John totally surprised me one morning, during our holiday in Folkestone, when he said he would like to show me the house that he grew up in. He rarely ever spoke of his childhood and never of his parents. It seemed such a shame, but he was so wonderfully kind is so many respects that I never questioned him as I knew if he wanted to share anything with me then he certainly would.

And so, we made our way to 21 Darby Road Folkestone. The house was at the end of a long terrace adjacent to patch of land that was in front of the train line to Dover. It had a bay front window and two first floor front windows. John said it had three bedrooms and he lived there with his grandmother Eliza his mother Emily and his uncle Charles. He did not mention his father at all. He stood outside the house for quite a long while just staring at it. Obviously, there was lots and lots rumbling around in his head. Lots of reminiscing.

After a few minutes, he simply said, "OK, let's go." We walked up the road in silence and made our way back towards the town centre. As we walked along Coolinge Road, all of a sudden, he said let's do a little detour. We turned right and went up Brockman Road. To my astonishment, he then announced – look, this is my old school. It was in those days Christ Church School. Here he seemed to have happier memories as his face lit up. He went on to say that it was here that he first played football. He was in the school team and absolutely loved it. This passion for footie remained with him always.

We had such a lovely holiday touring around the area. Folkestone was charming and we also visited Dover and Hythe. We were lucky with the weather and it stayed nice and warm for us and amazingly, no rain. Considering the awful previous winter weather, having sunshine and warmth was welcomed.

A highlight of the holiday was a trip on the Romney, Hythe and Dymchurch Railway. This is a 15 in (381 mm) gauge light railway in operating steam and internal combustion locomotives. The 13 3⁄4-mile (22.1 km) line runs from the Cinque Port of Hythe via Dymchurch, St Mary's Bay, New Romney and Romney Sands to Dungeness and Dungeness Lighthouse.

It has been around since 1927 and known as the smallest public railway in the world.

It was the most wonderful experience. The steam engine and carriages are much smaller than normal and such fun to travel on. To get on and off you needed to make sure that you bobbed your head, or you would end up bashing yourself. The carriages were tiny, and it was a tad cramped but that added to the fun.

We got on at Hythe and slowly made our way chugging along toward Dungeness. The journey time was just over an hour. Once there we had the opportunity to get off and have a wander around the beautiful area. Dungeness is one of the largest expanses of shingle in the world and is classified as Britain's only desert by the met office. We had lunch at the station café and, all too soon, we were getting back on the train again and heading the opposite way back to Hythe. Susan got overly excited each time the whistle blew and had the most amazing time.

To John's utter delight, one of the coaches even had a small bar. He was able to have one of his beloved beers. Mind you, he could only have half a pint in a pint pot. The reason being is that the carriages moved around so much when on the go, a full pint would end up being spilled all over the place.

It genuinely was a wonderful experience. Such fun. It is still going today, and I expect that if I went back, I would find that it had not changed at all. If you get the chance, you should visit. It is the most extraordinary experience.

Photos from our holiday in Folkestone – August 1963

Christmas 1963 was wonderful. We spent it at home and celebrated together. Susan received a toy from us that Christmas which was a battery-operated mechanical clown playing drums and it had a bright red flashing nose. John would walk down the corridor, in the dark, and all you could see was the red nose flashing and hear the drums clattering. Susan absolutely loved it and played with it for hours and hours.

Following New Year, on 22nd January, was Susan's seventh birthday. John bought her birthday card and, as he usually did, signed it from both of us. Even in a simple birthday card, John used the most amazing words. I kept the card as the words were so lovely and I felt it should be treasured.

Hello! You ARE 7 To-DAY Happy Birthday!

HERE'S A GREETING FOR
YOUR BIRTHDAY
SENT SPECIALLY TO YOU
WISHING YOU EVERY
HAPPINESS
EACH HOUR THE WHOLE
DAY THROUGH!

To Darling Susan, on this
Auspicious Occasion, with
all our blessings and Eternal
love. Dad and Mum
X X X X X X X.

Chapter 28

The following month on 17 February, we celebrated my 44th birthday.

A couple of weeks after my birthday, our lives were to change forever. My dearest darling or darlings, my beloved John was all of a sudden seriously ill. He was in tremendous pain and we had no choice but to call for an ambulance. He was taken immediately to Westminster Hospital in Central London. After numerous tests, they advised that he had pancreatic cancer. This is one of the most lethal malignancies and, as in John's case, not detected until at an advanced stage. Nothing could be done, and it was now a waiting game though they said he was not long for this world. He was never to return home.

John died peacefully on 22nd March 1964.

I could not believe he had been taken from me all too soon. What was I to do? How would I manage? I was in a terrible state. Poppy and George were aware of John's illness and when he died, I immediately called them. Straight away, they were in their car and drove up to London to be with us and help with all that would need to be done.

Although I was a consummate professional and able to deal with any eventuality; in this instance, Poppy took over and made all the necessary arrangements. The first thing on the agenda was to call the Admiralty to locate Gary and let him know his father had died. Gary was on deployment on a ship in the Far East, but the Royal Navy flew him back straight away. He arrived only four days after John had died in full uniform with his kitbag over his shoulder. In those days, military personnel were always in full uniform off base. Gary arrived in his white uniform and with either five or seven horizontal creases on his trousers. I cannot remember how many he had but tradition was five or seven creases depending on your height. They signified the five oceans or seven seas.

He looked incredibly smart indeed, and had already decided that he would wear his full uniform for the funeral. I was not sure how he would be with me but actually, he was kind and understanding. I suppose it helped that Poppy and

George were there too. Gary was wonderful with Susan and they became good friends. Susan became very fond of him.

The following morning, I gave Susan a cup of tea to take to Gary. She was extremely nervous about carrying a cup and saucer with hot tea, but I purposely did not fill it up to the top. Being especially cautious she walked the few feet from kitchen to the lounge. I tapped on the door for her and opened it. Gary was sleeping on the sofa in the lounge. I let her in then closed the door again. A few minutes later she came back looking perplexed. Of course, I asked her what was wrong, and she blurted out that Gary was not wearing pyjamas, only boxer shorts. Susan was used to seeing her dad all covered up with pyjamas. Also, Gary was full of tattoos.

At a time of such sorrow, Susan made me smile as she explained that Gary was painted all over. Actually, his torso and arms were covered in tattoos. He had a large pirate type ship/galleon on his chest, with seagulls flying around in the sky, and sharks in the sea. Geisha girls on his arms, and hearts. There was quite a lot more, but I cannot remember any longer. She had been utterly mesmerised by his painted body.

It was at this time that I discovered John's actual age. As mentioned earlier in my story, when I met him, I understood he had been born in 1905. However, in order to register his death, I needed to obtain a copy of his birth certificate. I had gone through his papers but there was no certificate. Poppy again helped with this and she sent George to Somerset House in Central London where, at the time, the records for all births, deaths and marriages are kept, to obtain a copy. When he got back and handed it over to me, to my surprise, it showed that John had been born on 19th April 1907 – so he was two years younger than I had thought. This made him only 56 years old when he died – so no age at all.

On John's death certificate the cause of death was noted as pancreatic cancer and shock.

A small funeral was arranged. I decided that Susan was too young to attend so she stayed with Mrs Wilkins. The day went as well as one could expect under the circumstances. I needed to keep my composure for Susan and Marietta, but it was not in the least an easy task. I was utterly heartbroken that my one true love had been taken from me. I truly began to question my faith. Why should this have happened? There had already been enough tragedy in my life, why should I be given more to contend with? It all seem so unjust.

John was buried on 28th March 1964, at the Lambeth Cemetery, Blackshaw Road, in Tooting, South London. I bought a double plot with the intention that when my time comes, I will be interred with him and we will be together once again.

Lambeth Cemetery, Blackshaw Road, Tooting, S.W.17

CONSECRATED GROUND

Name of Deceased   John Nicholson CROWLEY.

Date of Burial   28th March, 1964.

No. of Grave   98&   M 2nd.   Consecrated Purchased.

(PLEASE SEE OTHER SIDE)

M378

I could not comprehend how I was going to manage on my own, in a still relatively strange country with two young daughters. But I had got through the most awful circumstances in the past and I had to be strong for my two precious girls.

Initially, I took over John's role as the caretaker for the flats. It was not what I wanted to do but I needed to work and keep busy.

But one day whilst in the office alone, a man came in demanding I hand over the rent monies. He was brandishing a knife and acting menacingly. I was terrified and instantly gave him the cash. It was not much and definitely was not worthwhile arguing over.

This incident truly scared me, and I knew that I could not carry on in this role. Therefore, I resigned. Thankfully, my decision was understood. We had to give up the caretaker's flat but luckily, there was an empty flat in the same block that we could move in to straight away. So, we moved up to the third floor into 43 Atholl Mansions.

One good thing to come out of the move was that finally, Marietta had her own bedroom which she was absolutely thrilled about. The first thing on the agenda was to buy her a proper bed and get rid of the folding bed which she truly hated.

Susan was still young, so she slept with me.

John had served for so long that he was entitled to an army pension and, on his death, it passed to me. This would help our financial situation, but I needed to get a job. My secretarial skills would have to become useful again. Life would never be the same. I missed my soulmate so very much, but I now had to focus on Marietta and Susan.

My dearest darling John

And so here, I finish my tale. I hope you enjoyed reading it.

I do not want to end this narrative on a sad note, so the following is something I found in John's possessions after he had died. I have no idea who wrote it originally, or when it was written, but it is incredibly funny. Often, I come across it and even after all these years, it still makes me smile and remember my dearest darling John.

Alcoholic's Lament

I had 18 bottles of whisky in my cellar and was told by my wife to empty the contents of each and every bottle down the sink, OR ELSE.

I said I would and proceeded with the unpleasant task. I withdrew the cork from the first bottle and poured the contents down the sink, with exception of one glass, which I drank.

I extracted the cork from the second bottle and did likewise with it, with the exception of one glass, which I drank.

I then withdrew the cork from the third bottle and poured the whisky down the sink, which I drank.

I pulled the cork from the fourth bottle down the sink, and poured the bottle down the glass, which I drank.

I pulled the bottle from the cork of the next and drank one sink out of it, and threw the rest down the glass.

I pulled the sink out of the next glass and poured the cork down the bottle. Then I corked the sink with the glass, bottled the drink and drank the pour. When I had everything emptied, I steadied the house with one hand, counted the corks, bottles, glasses and sinks with the other and found there were twenty-nine. As the house came by I counted them again and finally had all the house in one bottle, which I drank.

I am not under the affluence of incohol as some tinkle peep. I am not thunk as you might drink. I fool feelish. I don't know who I am, who is me and the drunker I stand here the longer I get, but I wish someone would keep this house still.

Source: Donald Tsang – netfunny.com